MITZI CLARK

&

THE KEEPERS OF

SHUT

Grace Mirchandani

D1527556

First Edition, 2021
Published in the United States

Editing: Genevieve A. Scholl
Cover Design: Sinisa Poznanovic

TABLE OF CONTENTS

DEDICATION

For Roe, Ronan, Logan, and Emmy.

Thank you for being my constant source of inspiration.

CHAPTER ONE

Mitzi sat at her bedroom desk, strumming her fingers against the wood surface. It was only two weeks into summer vacation, and she was already bored. She didn't want to watch television or read a book. She spent most of the winter doing those things, and she was craving an adventure. But what kind of an adventure could a twelve-year-old girl have while living in the middle of nowhere?

She pushed a strand of her shoulder-length brown hair away from her face and sighed. Her eyes searched the fields outside through the bedroom window, desperate to find a solution to her boredom.

Nothing.

No birds to watch. Not even a breeze.

Just a big, grassy field that stretched about half a mile to the edge of a forest. *Well, at least it's sunny outside. Finally, a break from all the dang rain*, she thought. That was reason enough to leave the confines of her room.

She stood up and stretched her arms in an exaggerated yawn.

A flicker of bright light out of the corner of her eye brought her attention back to the window. She leaned over her desk and pressed her nose against the glass. Straining her eyes in an effort to focus on the source of the bright light, Mitzi noticed it seemed to be coming from the tree line at the edge of the field.

What could it be? she mused.

She scrambled back to the desk and jerked open the bottom drawer. After a few moments of searching for her new binoculars, a Christmas present from her father that she hadn't really used yet, she held them up to her face and turned the center dial to try to focus on the shiny object. But her excitement was making her hands dance around, rendering the image blurry and unfocused.

"Maybe it's just too far away," she said to herself out loud.

She shrugged her shoulders and sat on the end of her bed. *I guess I can go and see what it is*, she thought. *It's not like I have anything better to do, anyway*. She grabbed her oversized hoodie off the floor and headed downstairs, straight for the door.

"Mom! I'm going for a walk!" she yelled out as she pulled on her old rubber boots.

"Be back by noon for lunch!" her mom yelled back from the direction of the dining room. "And dress warm! It's still a little chilly out there!"

Mitzi rolled her eyes. *I'm not a baby anymore! Why does she always have to nag at me? At least outside, I can get away from her and have a tiny bit of space.*

Mitzi was tired of her hovering over her all the time. She was so overprotective! It was like they had nothing in common. Mitzi was level-headed and normal, and her mother was a bit strange.

She wasn't like all the other moms. She always wore the strangest clothes and large, clunky, colorful jewelry. The house was littered with what her mother called 'healing' crystals and smoking herbal blends, and she filled the kitchen counters with homemade herbs and tinctures that she was always forcing Mitzi to drink or wash her face with. She was always humming a strange tune or having conversations with herself. She was embarrassing!

Mitzi tried to keep her distance from her as much as possible, afraid that some of her weirdness may somehow rub off onto her.

At least her father was normal. He was never embarrassing. He was actually kind of cool. He was always so busy, though; working all the time. Sometimes Mitzi would go days without even seeing him even though he worked out of their home office. Mitzi often wondered why her two parents ever got married. Mostly, she wondered how a normal guy like her dad could end up with a nutter like her mom.

Mitzi pushed open the door, relieved to be leaving the house. At least outside, she could do her own thing without being bothered.

The sunshine felt nice on her face. The sky was bright blue and there wasn't a cloud in sight. The June morning air was unusually cool and crisp, and the ground was soft from recent rain.

Mitzi craned her neck around the house to try to get an unobstructed view of the tree line, but couldn't see the glimmer she saw from her window. Her steps quick with anticipation, she arrived at the edge of the forest in what felt like a flash.

"Now, where did that flicker come from?" she said to no one.

She bent down to the ground and picked up a very heavy rock that was about the size of a small watermelon. She placed it on top of a tree stump as a marker of her starting point, just in case she lost her way.

She walked along the edge, scanning the ground and looking waist high into the trees. It was slow work, and she moved just a few feet at a time, careful not to miss anything.

***

After about an hour of searching, she figured that she must have passed by the mysterious light source. She was discouraged and thought, *Forget this. I'm never going to find it. I don't even know what I'm looking for. Oh well.*

As she turned to head back home, her foot struck a hard object that made a metallic thud. "What the…" Her voice trailed off as she reached down to pick up the small, shiny metal box that was poking out of the ground.

It was stuck! She scraped the hard dirt around the edges, trying to free the treasure.

"UGH!" She let out a frustrated gasp.

She found a sturdy stick and made fast progress of digging away the dirt with its sharp edge. The box was free.

The little metal box was a simple one. It was polished and shiny even though it was buried in the dirt for who knows how long. On the bottom, the initials F.C. had been etched very crudely. Mitzi gave the box a little shake and was disappointed when it didn't make a sound. *Hhhhmmmmm. Maybe it's just an old little box? But then why bury it? Maybe there's some sort of letter inside…*

The rim around the edge of the box was very thin, and Mitzi had a difficult time prying the old lid off. She had to get her dirty fingernails just underneath the thin metal and twist and pull for several minutes. Finally, a *krrr-pop!* and the lid was free, revealing a faded blue velvet wad of fabric.

Her heart was racing as she removed the cloth and let the box fall to the ground. Something was wrapped inside. As quickly as she could, Mitzi unraveled the fabric and found a strange piece of metal. She was confused and sat on the ground to study it. It looked like it was made from silver. It was about six inches long and skinny on one end and flat on the other. The skinny end resembled the handle of an old skeleton key, like the kind of key that would open an old trunk or big old door. Again, the initials F.C. were decorated into the end but much more ornately.

The other end, the flat end, was just slightly larger than a quarter with two large notches removed from the edge, like little pie slices had been cut out. The bottom was ornately decorated with swirls and symbols that looked strangely familiar to Mitzi.

She sat and turned the treasure over and over in her hands, pondering its purpose.

I know I have seen this symbol somewhere before, but where? What the heck is this thing anyway? It can't be a key…the end is too flat so that wouldn't make sense. Maybe it's some kind of stamp or seal? I remember, in Social Studies, Mr. Creeker said that people used to use melted wax to seal letters and documents and stuff, and then stamp their seal into the wax. I bet that's what it is! But why hide it? Looks like I may have a bit of a mystery on my hands.

Mitzi smiled and wrapped the stamp back up in the velvet cloth and tucked it back inside the box. Standing and brushing the dust and dirt off her jeans, she crammed the box into her hoodie pocket and started back toward the farmhouse. She wondered who 'F.C' could be.

She stopped walking as she realized that it very well may have been a relative of hers. Her father always said the farm had been in the family for several generations, but Mitzi was never interested in hearing more about it. Until now.

She had a plan. After lunch, she would ask her father to tell her the story of their farm, and all the people who lived in it before. Hopefully, he had enough time to see her for a few minutes.

Chapter Two

Lunch was hot and spicy tomato soup with grilled cheese sandwiches, which Mitzi devoured in record time. She was so anxious to ask her father about the history of their home.

She stood in front of the big wood door that led to his office. She took a deep breath and held it, and knocked softly.

"Come on in!" came a soft voice from inside.

Mitzi stepped into the office and saw her father sitting in a large green armchair by the window, reading from a clipboard and sipping from a steaming mug. The air smelled like stale pipe tobacco and the room was slightly dark with sun beams streaming in through the window and landing across her father's paperwork.

He was a handsome man. Medium height with dark hair that was always a little messy, and he kept a short, scruffy beard. He wore black, round metal framed glasses that sat low on his nose, and he always wore a button-down dress shirt even when he was working from home. He was some kind of lawyer, but Mitzi didn't really know much about that.

"Hey, Dad." Mitzi smiled. "I was wondering if you had a minute. I have some questions that I thought you might be able to help me with."

Her father set down the clipboard and looked at her curiously. "I have a few minutes before my next client call." He looked worried. "Is everything alright?"

"Oh! Yeah… yeah…it's nothing important!" Mitzi felt her cheeks flush red. "I was just curious about this house and the people who lived here before us."

"Well, okay then." He motioned for her to sit in the small brown chair across from him. "What would you like to know?"

Mitzi looked around the office as she sat. The walls were covered with framed old maps, certificates, and tapestries. The shelves were filled with old books and strange looking trinkets. The giant, old desk was messy with folders and papers piled up and scattered.

"You are always saying that our family has lived here for generation after generation. Well…how long ago was that? Do you know who they were and why they picked this place? I mean, it's kind of in the middle of nowhere…" Mitzi shrugged and shifted in her chair.

"My grandfather actually had this house built back in 1920. He settled here as an immigrant from London. He decided to move to America to start a new law firm here. I'm not really sure why he chose to build this house in such a remote place but I'm sure he had his reasons. Why the sudden interest, anyway?" He tilted his head and looked at Mitzi, waiting for her reply.

"Oh, I don't know," she lied. "It just hit me suddenly that I didn't know anything about my ancestry and got a bit interested, I guess."

"That makes sense. Any other questions, young lady?" He smiled.

"Yeah, just one." She cleared her throat. "What was his name?"

"My grandfather's name was Frederick Clark. But I can do better than just give you his name." His statement piqued Mitzi's curiosity again. "There is a huge portrait of him hanging in the guest bedroom upstairs."

With that, Mitzi stood and hollered, "Thanks, Pop!" as she sped to exit the office.

"I don't see what the big deal is, kid." Her dad chuckled as he yelled after her. "It's been hanging on that wall for a hundred years...I don't think it's going anywhere anytime soon."

Mitzi's excitedly took the stairs two at a time. Her mind was racing as she walked down the hall toward the guest room.

Frederick Clark!!! F.C. were his initials! The silver stamp must have belonged to him! My great-grandfather! But why on earth would he have buried it in an old box at the edge of the forest? Maybe he just lost it, and it slowly got buried over the decades? Who knows?

Mitzi entered the guest room and couldn't help but hold her breath. The large portrait hung directly across the room from the door and as she walked closer, she was drawn to her great-grandfather's eyes. They looked so much like her father's eyes. But why shouldn't they? The oil painting was housed in a wide, gold frame.

Frederick Clark had an expression on his face that suggested he was bored or at least very serious. His hair was dark, neat, and parted on one side. He had a thick mustache and a long-pointed nose. He was wearing a dark blue coat and holding a silver pocket watch. *Wow. He looks like he was quite a fancy guy. But why is he holding a pocket watch? Maybe it was a popular thing to do back then? But what if it's significant?* Mitzi leaned closer to the painting to get a better look at the watch.

She squinted her eyes to focus on the face of the pocket watch. The long hand was pointed to the seven and the shorthand was on the three. *I wonder if that means anything? 3:35…hmm…I better start writing this stuff down. Maybe it's just the time the painter of the portrait decided to paint? Seems strange to have the watch held in such a way that it even shows the face of the watch, though. It MUST be significant…. but how?*

Mitzi wasn't really sure what to do next. She went to her bedroom and got an empty notebook and started writing down her clues.

She plopped down on her bed and stared up at the ceiling. *It's only a stamp. Maybe there is no big mystery at all. You are always making a big deal out of nothing. I should just stop this stupidity now. But then why bury the thing?!*

That was the one detail that kept the mystery swirling in Mitzi's mind. *I should call Rose. Maybe she will have some ideas…I should call Finn, too. Maybe the three of us can figure this out together.*

Chapter Three

The doorbell rang, and Mitzi ran down the stairs like her pants were on fire and a pool of water was at the bottom. She was surprised when she opened the door to find Mr. Moore, their elderly neighbor, instead of her anticipated friends.

"Good afternoon, young lady," he said with a smile.

"Hello, Mr. Moore. How are you today?" Mitzi motioned for him to come into the house.

"Oh, well…you know, this old grey mare just ain't what he used to be!" He chuckled. "Takes me twice as long to do half of what I used to…but at 90 years old, I guess I really can't complain." He started hobbling toward the kitchen. "Is your ma back there?"

"I think so," Mitzi answered although she really wasn't sure at all.

Mr. Moore lived just a couple miles away. He was the only neighbor who lived within ten miles of the family home. He stopped by everyday around three o'clock for tea since his wife Maude passed away three years ago. Mitzi liked the old man. He often told her funny stories about the past, and he was the king of the super cheesy joke. It didn't bother Mitzi that he would tell the same joke again and again because he was kind. He was lonely, and Mitzi was happy to be an occasional friend. He had a hard time hearing, his vision wasn't so great, he would often fall asleep without warning, and his false teeth were always sliding out of his mouth.

Sometimes, he would get frustrated with his false teeth coming loose and would just pull them out of his mouth and cram them into his pocket. With a toothless snarl, he would yell out, "To HELL with it!" Then he would proceed to suck his cheeks in and out and make funny faces at Mitzi. He was a real hoot, and Mitzi enjoyed his daily visits.

But today, she didn't want to join her mom and Mr. Moore in the kitchen. She was too excited for the arrival of her friends and could hardly wait to brainstorm a plan to solve the mystery of the buried stamp.

Mitzi started pacing the front hall while waiting for her friends. Growing increasingly impatient, she decided to wait for them on the big front porch that wrapped around the sides of the old house. As she pulled open the big front door, she was startled by her friends standing there. Rose's hand was stretched in front of her, and she was just about to press the doorbell.

"Oh!" Mitzi exclaimed with a giant smile on her face.

"Surprise! We are here." Rose giggled, and Finn pushed his glasses up his nose with his pointer finger.

Rose was a pretty girl. Her skin was the color of coffee with cream and her eyes were large and golden brown. She was slightly taller than Mitzi, and had a very athletic build. She kept her black hair in long braids that had pink and purple streaks running through them. She cared a lot about the latest clothing trends and always looked like she was ready to take a selfie, even if she was only going to the grocery store.

Finn was the opposite of Rose. He was thin as a rail and extremely pale. He had the lightest blond hair, and it was usually a crumpled mess. He wore dark, plastic glasses that were always sliding down his nose. His clothes always looked a little too big on him and pretty worn out. They were hand-me-downs from his two older brothers who were obviously and considerably bigger than he was. He didn't seem to mind, though. Or, if he did, he didn't say anything. Of course, he never said much. He was quiet most of the time but incredibly smart.

The three of them met on school bus number nine. They all rode that bus on the first day of kindergarten and sat next to each other, and had been sitting in those same seats ever since.

The three had become even closer in the sixth grade when the drama club put on *The Wizard of Oz*. Rose was cast as Dorothy, the leading role. Mitzi was selected to play the flute in the orchestra, and Finn was part of the tech crew. They spent so much time together during the eight weeks of rehearsals that the trio became like a little family. It was just so easy to be around each other.

"Well, that was some good timing right there…" Mitzi motioned them inside. "Come in, come in! Let's head up to my room." The three sounded like a herd of wild elephants racing up the steps to Mitzi's room.

"So, what's the news on the farm, girl?" Rose asked as she sat cross legged on the bedroom floor.

"Oh, I cannot wait to show you what I found!" Mitzi grinned.

Finn sat on the corner of the bed, looking at Mitzi with a curious look of anticipation. Mitzi pulled her notebook and the box from the desk drawer and held the unidentified thing up for them to see. Mitzi rattled off the story of her morning walk, her strange discovery, and the conversation she had with her father. The two sat wide-eyed and listened without interruption.

"So," Mitzi took a slow breath, winded from talking so quickly, "I want to see if we can find out more about the symbol on the stamp, what it was used for, and if the time on the portrait of my great-grandfather means anything."

"Why do you think it means anything at all?" Rose questioned. "It's just a stamp, right?"

"I thought about that a lot." Mitzi sighed. "If it is *only* a stamp, then why bury it in a secret location? It feels more important than that. I just have a feeling that it means something!"

Finn cleared his throat. "I think the first thing we should do is search the house and grounds for any other clues…then we could all research on the internet about this address and this F.C. guy and see what we come up with."

"Sounds like a good plan." Mitzi grinned from ear to ear. "We aren't allowed in my dad's office, and my mom and Mr. Moore are in the kitchen, but we can search everywhere else."

"I don't get it," said Rose. "What exactly are we looking for? I mean, Mitzi, you have lived here your whole life. If there was something to find, don't you think you would have found it already? You do have a tendency to create drama out of nothing."

"Hmmm." Mitzi considered her thoughts. "Well, my dad used to say that the hardest things to find are the things right in front of your face. Plus, what do we have to lose? You have better things to do today, Rose?"

Finn pushed his glasses up his nose. "I don't know about you, Rose, but I don't have crap to do today." He smiled. "This might be fun."

Rose shrugged her shoulders and stood up. "Where do we start?"

Deep in thought, Mitzi tapped her pencil on her chin. "Let's start in the basement and work our way up to the attic. That way we don't miss anything. But, guys…let's keep this a secret. I don't want my mom and dad to spoil our fun."

"Ugh. The basement is going to kill me. All that musty dampness." Finn grumbled as he pulled his arm across his face to wipe his nose with his sleeve. "Thank God my mom gave me my allergy meds today."

"For the love of God! Get a tissue, Finny!" Rose looked grossed out.

"I'll get you some to take with you on our mission." Mitzi chuckled. "I'll grab each of us a flashlight, too."

She looked at her friends and raised her eyebrows in excitement. "Let's do this!"

CHAPTER FOUR

"AAAHHHHHH-

CCCCCCHHHHHHOOOOOOOOO!!!"

Finn sneezed for what seemed like the hundredth time in ten minutes. The basement was dark and musty. There were no windows and only one light in the center of the very large room. It was a bare lightbulb hanging from a cord, and it turned on by pulling a chain. The trio was glad to have their flashlights as the single bulb's light didn't even come close to reaching the walls and corners of the room. The floor was damp dirt, and the walls were rock and mud. Other than the annoying sneezes, the three searched in silence for a few minutes.

"There's nothing here but cobwebs and dirt," complained Rose.

"I agree with Rose," Finn said with a congested, whiny voice. "Perhaps, we should move on from here."

"Right," agreed Mitzi. "But let's split up. Finn, you check the hall bathroom and Rose and I will check the living room. We can meet in the kitchen for a snack in ten minutes. In the kitchen, we can do our best to look around for anything obvious at least."

"Mitzi?" said Finn. "What do we do if we are questioned about snooping around? You know, by one of your parents?"

Mitzi turned the flashlight on Finn's face, and he squinted his eyes as he waited for her answer.

Rose chimed in, "Well, that's easy… just tell them that we are looking for your new cell phone."

"But I don't have a cellphone." Finn shrugged.

"I guess we will be looking a long time then, huh?" Rose giggled.

"Brilliant." Mitzi took the stairs two at a time again, excited to get back into the fresh air of the house and continue their search.

***

The living room was a large, rectangular room with a brick fireplace opposite from the door. Above the fireplace was a large, old-looking oil painting of a bunch of fruit and flowers. The wall space on the sides of the fireplace held dozens and dozens of old books.

"Let's start our search at the fireplace and work our way back to the door." Mitzi looked at Rose for her approval.

Rose nodded, and the two started their search.

Nothing seemed out of the ordinary at the fireplace. The books on the shelves were old and dusty but otherwise just books. Rose searched the right wall, which was mostly big, old windows with white lace curtains, and Mitzi searched the left wall. The left wall was plain with a large, oval mirror in the center with a wall sconce on either side of it and a small table centered underneath it. The wood floor creaked and moaned underneath their feet as they worked toward the middle of the room, each examining the furniture along the way.

"I don't see anything interesting here either." Mitzi shrugged.

"Nope. Just a room," Rose said with a tone of boredom.

The girls turned as Finn burst into the room.

"You guys need to see this!" His eyes were wide with excitement. "You're never going to believe what I found in the bathroom."

The three practically ran to the small bathroom across from the kitchen.

"So, I was almost ready to give up the search and then I thought I should take a better look behind the cabinet." He pointed to an old wooden cabinet that held towels and toiletries. "It wasn't easy, you know. It's old and pretty heavy…and I'm not the strongest…but I managed to pull it out…then I had to put it back before I came to get you…and it was dusty, too…and I…"

"Oh, for goodness sake!" interrupted Rose. "Show us what you found already!"

"The suspense is killing me!" Mitzi bounced up and down as she started to pull at the cabinet.

"So, the wall behind the cabinet, as you can see, is brick." Finn looked proud of himself. "At first, I thought there was nothing here but then I got on my hands and knees and saw *that* in the lower corner." He pointed down and to the right.

Both girls dropped to their hands and knees and brought their faces close to the wall. Etched into one of the bricks, was a circle with a fancy letter 'G' and the number '5' carved inside of it.

"Oh my God, that's so cool," Mitzi whispered.

"Heck yeah it is," agreed Rose. "I honestly didn't think we would find anything at all if I'm being real with you."

"The most important question is…what does it mean?" Finn looked from girl to girl.

"I don't know, but now we *definitely* have a real mystery on our hands and I can't wait to figure this out!" Mitzi jumped up and down with excitement as a mischievous grin washed over her face. "I think for now we had better get out of the bathroom… before my mom starts wondering why the three of us are in here together."

They laughed as they headed into the kitchen to grab a snack. Well…to grab a snack and to look for more clues, of course.

CHAPTER FIVE

"How do you get a handkerchief to dance?" Mr. Moore questioned the kids as they sat at the table eating apple slices and peanut butter.

"We don't know...how?" Finn mumbled through a mouth full of apples.

"You put a little BOOGIE in it!" Mr. Moore slapped the table and chuckled to himself.

Rose rolled her eyes and looked over at Mitzi, who giggled a polite giggle. Mr. Moore loved telling silly jokes to anyone that would listen. The problem was that he had a bad memory and would often tell the same joke again and again. The group had heard that joke at least five times, but they enjoyed sitting with Mr. Moore and hearing his old stories.

Mitzi's mom, Deb, was busy lighting a bundle of dried sage at the counter and humming a strange little tune to herself. She was tall and thin with long black hair that she always had swooped into a messy bun. She was a pretty woman, with large dark-brown eyes and a kind smile. She walked around the table with her smokestack of sage, filling the room with thick, pungent smoke.

"Mom, do you really need to do that *now*?" Mitzi coughed and rolled her eyes. "It stinks!"

"Hey, Mitzo." She stopped and extinguished the smoldering herbs in the sink. "A little spiritual cleansing never hurt no one. Sage burning clears all the negative energy right out of our home."

"That smells so bad it's going to clear *me* right out of our home," Mitzi teased.

"Well, don't go too far," Deb said. "I happen to like you. By the way, I'm going to run into town in a few minutes to grab some stuff for tonight."

"What's happening tonight?" Mitzi asked.

"Dad has some business associates stopping by to go over a case they've been working on. Your friends are welcome to hang, but you'll need to stay upstairs and out of sight for a while." She turned to face them.

"That's cool, Ma. We can hang out in my room."

Mitzi thought it might actually be a great chance to search the attic!

"I can grab a pizza for you guys while I'm in town, but right now I need to get cleaned up so I can get a move on it." Deb walked toward the kitchen doorway and turned to face the group. "Have a nice day, Mr. Moore. Please try that sesame seed paste I mixed you for your bad knees. I will see you tomorrow."

"Only if I live that long!" He smiled and waved from his seat at the table as Deb headed upstairs to get ready.

Rose's face flashed a look of realization and she sat up in her chair. "Mr. Moore?" she spoke softly. "How long have you lived next door, anyway?"

"I have lived down the road my whole life!" he said as he leaned forward in his chair. "My pa built the house back in 1918 when he and Ma moved here from Europe. In fact, this house and my house were two of the first homes built on the outskirts of town."

"I heard you were friends with my grandpa, Mr. Moore, but did you know his father at all?" Mitzi had a serious look on her face.

"I knew old man Clark as much as any kid could really know him, I guess." He chuckled. "He was stern and serious most of the time… didn't really interact with us kids…"

He paused. "It was a different time back then. Adults and kids didn't really interact with each other the way they do today. Your grandpa Morty and I used to hang out at the old cabin most of the time."

"What's the old cabin?" Finn asked curiously.

"You wouldn't know about that, would you?" Mr. Moore scratched his chin. "They burned that old place down when the roof started to crumble back in the 1940s... or was it in the 1950s? Hmmm… Anywho." Mr. Moore lost his train of thought and sat quietly staring off into the distance. He was starting to doze off.

"Mr. Moore?" Rose asked. "You were telling us about the cabin…"

"What about a rabbit?" Mr. Moore startled himself awake and looked confused.

"No. The cabin!" Finn tried to hide his laugh, but giggled a bit anyway.

"You were about to tell us about the cabin you and Grandpa used to hang out in," said Mitzi.

"Oh. Right. I knew that." Mr. Moore adjusted himself in his chair again. "Well, back in the day, when we were young whippersnappers like you three here, we used to play in the old builder's cabin in the back by the stream." He thrusted his thumb behind his shoulder, pointing it toward the back of the house. "We would play cards and shoot our slingshots and try to catch fish in the stream. We climb trees and build campfires and that kind of thing."

"Did you ever catch any fish?" Finn asked.

Mitzi shot Finn an irritated look. She didn't care about the fish. She wanted to learn more about the cabin!

"We caught a few fish here and there, but I can honestly tell you that we weren't the best fisherman in the world. They were never big enough to keep and eat, that's for sure."

"Why was it called a builder's cabin?" Mitzi asked. "What was it like?"

"Oh." Mr. Moore looked at Mitzi. "It was a small rustic log cabin that the builders and workers lived in while the farm was being built. It was just one big room, really. Your great grandfather hired people to help do the building with him, so he and the other men lived in there, and when the house was ready, he sent for your great granny and then they moved into the main house. The cabin had two sets of wooden bunks, a table, and a small stove in the corner. That's it. Nothing fancy at all." Mr. Moore was looking tired.

"I wish it was still there," Mitzi said.

"Yeah. That would be so cool," agreed Finn.

Rose looked excited. "We should go see where it was!"

"Yep. You should," said Mr. Moore. "Kids these days never get any fresh air. Your dad has a big ol' map of the property hanging up somewhere around here, I think. It shows the spot the old cabin was on."

Mitzi knew exactly where the map was hanging. It was in her father's office, but there was no way they would be able to look at it today because of his business meeting... but she *could* ask him in the morning.

"Well, kiddos...it's been fun chit chatting with you, but I need to be on my way." Mr. Moore slowly stood up from his chair, grabbed his jar of sesame paste, and started shuffling out toward the door. "See you tomorrow, Mitz."

"Bye, Mr. Moore!" the three called out in unison.

Rose looked from Finn to Mitzi. "So, now what do we do?"

"I say we get online and see what we can find out about old F.C.," suggested Finn.

"That's what I was just about to say," said Mitzi with a smile as the three of them stood and headed upstairs.

CHAPTER SIX

The three hovered around Mitzi's laptop, trying their best to find out any information about F.C. or the history of the home. The only thing they were able to find after an hour of searching was the town of Hadford's Historic Society website. There was an article about early construction practices that mentioned the Clark House and the Builder's cabin. There was a photo of the old cabin with the caption: **Clark's Builder's Cabin sits empty decades after completion of the home, 1948. Demolished by planned fire in 1953.**

"Well, at least we got to see what it looked like." Rose stretched her arms above her head as she yawned.

"It's pretty cool, I think," said Finn. "We totally need to go find the spot and see if we can find anything there."

"I agree," added Mitzi. "I don't know if that old cabin was anything other than an old cabin, but it might be fun to check it out anyway." Mitzi shrugged.

Rose got a mischievous look on her face. "I say, we sneak up to the attic and peek around there for a bit."

Mitzi walked over to look out her bedroom window. There were three cars parked on the gravel driveway, so Mitzi knew her father was busy in his meeting and wouldn't be done for quite a while. Her mother was buzzing around town doing *her* thing, and Mitzi knew if they were going to go snooping upstairs undetected now would be the time to do it.

"Let's do it." She grinned. "But we need to be as quiet as a thief in a museum."

As quietly as possible, the three tiptoed to the attic door at the end of the hall upstairs. The door creaked softly, and the detectives held their breaths as they listened to make sure they weren't discovered by the noise before making their way up the old narrow steps. Mitzi turned an old light switch at the top of the stairs and was surprised when the lights came on in the large room. The ceiling was exposed with wood roof beams and the walls were unfinished. The attic had an old book kind of smell, and was filled with boxes and tote bins.

"Where do we even start?" Rose looked from side to side of the room with a look of overwhelm on her face.

"Yeah, this is a lot of stuff," Finn added as he wiped his nose with his sleeve again.

"Well," Mitzi paused to think for a moment, "it seems like most of these containers are labeled. So, let's just look for things that are not labeled, or for anything that is obviously interesting."

As they searched through the contents, each would say out loud what was written on the containers ... *Christmas Decorations* ... *Winter Gear* ... *Grandmother's Clothes* ... *Sports Equipment* ... *Tax Documents* ... *Misc. Electrical cords* ... it all seemed like pretty normal attic stuff.

Finn suddenly stood up straight and tilted his head to the side. "Do you hear that?" he asked.

Rose shrugged. "Hear what?"

"I think I hear men talking. Shhhhh. Listen." He cupped his hand to his ear.

Mitzi looked puzzled. How could they hear her father and the other men in the attic when they were way down on the first floor? She moved over to where Finn was standing, and could hear the muffled voices, too. That was when she noticed a metal grate in the wall. It looked like it was made from cast iron. She kneeled down closer to the grate to see if she could hear the voices better.

"Well, I don't really think we need to open a new case for this, Thomas." Her father's voice sounded annoyed.

"Oh! Would you listen to reason!!!" another man's voice snapped back in frustrated tones. "Martin is MISSING! I don't think it's a coincidence that he went missing right after starting his investigation on the Halbert…"

"STOP!!!" a third man's voice interrupted. "Do not break the code! We never discuss a SHUT case in the open. Only in the DEN. You *know* that!"

"You are right, Logan." Her father's voice sounded tired. "We will finish this discussion in the

DEN. I do believe that dinner is waiting, and we will be able to think more clearly after we have had something to eat."

The voices coming through the grate fell silent. It was silent in the attic as well. The three stood wide eyed as they struggled to make sense of the overheard conversation.

Mitzi's mind raced. *What did we just overhear? Who was this Martin, and why is he missing? What investigation was he on? What code was he talking about? What is the DEN? That didn't sound like lawyers talking about a regular case. What the heck is going on?*

Finn broke the silence. "Well, that was a bit strange."

"Sure the heck was!" agreed Rose. "What was *that* all about, anyway? I thought your dad was some kind of business lawyer."

"Yes, he is," Mitzi answered defensively.

"Well, that did not sound like any regular lawyer talk to me," replied Rose.

"I know. I know. It was weird. Right now, though, we gotta get out of here before my mom finds us up here and starts asking questions!" Mitzi grabbed Finn as she passed him heading toward the stairs.

"Wait for me, guys!" Rose grumbled as she followed after them. They shut the attic door as quietly as they could and heard footsteps just starting up the main stairs.

"Hurry!" Mitzi mouthed in frantic silence as the three tip-toe-ran to Mitzi's room. They flew inside and sat down as quickly as they could as the bedroom door was being opened behind them.

"Who is hungry for some pizza?" Mitzi's mom asked as she stepped into the room with a big box in her hands. Mitzi's mom looked down at the group as the smile on her face faded to a look of suspicious curiosity. "What are you three little bears up to, anyway?" She tilted her head to the side.

"We aren't up to anything. Just chillin' and chattin', Ma." Mitzi sounded annoyed.

"Well, okay then. Best to keep it that way. I'll bring up some drinks in a little bit but otherwise I'm hoping I can trust the three of you to stay out of trouble." She looked at each one of them in turn with a very motherly look on her face.

"Yes, ma'am. No trouble at all," Finn squeaked out.

Rose nodded, and Mitzi chuckled to herself. "Hey Mom?"

"What's up, Mitz?" said Deb.

"Can Finn and Rose crash here tonight?" Mitzi asked.

"Oh, Mitzi. Dad has his big meeting, and I don't know how long it will go and…"

"Oh, but Mom, you haven't heard a peep out of us and we will keep it that way. We promise," Mitzi pleaded. "But we want to go check out where the old builder's cabin was…in the morning…and we won't be any trouble…please? Please? Please?"

"Oh alright. Alright," she relented. "But Finny, you sleep in the guestroom. You know the rule." She smiled as she opened the door to leave. "I want lights out by eleven! A rested soul is the bestest soul!"

"Whatever you say, Ma!" hollered Mitzi as she shook her head in embarrassment.

"Yeah. Thank you, Mrs. Clark!" giggled Rose.

"I guess we are spending the night then?" Finn grinned from ear to ear. "Well, that is, assuming that *our* parents say that it's okay."

"Well, you guys know my parents don't care if I stay." Rose looked at her feet. "I have practically lived here for the last three years."

"I know it totally sucks that your parents split up but at least they never say no to you anymore." Mitzi smiled at her best friend.

"That's true." Rose smiled. "Do you think I am wasting it all on sleepovers, though? Maybe it's time I ask for something *big*…like a shopping spree…or professional photo shoot?"

"Oh brother!" Finn complained. "I really need to get some guy friends."

Mitzi snatched a pillow from her bed and chucked it at Finn, hitting him square in the face. "Whatever, Finny." Mitzi laughed. "You'd be lost without us."

Chapter Seven

"Hey, you two lazy girls!" Finn called from the open doorway. "Would you get out of bed already so we can go…"

"Ugh, FINN!!!" Rose complained in a sleepy and noticeably irritated snarl. "Why do you gotta wake us up? It's summer, for cryin' out loud."

"We're up…we're up." Mitzi grumbled as she sat up in bed and rubbed her eyes. "We'll meet you in the kitchen in ten minutes."

"Okay. But hurry up! I'd like to get outside *before* it starts raining." Finn sighed and turned to head off downstairs.

"I think that boy needs to learn how to relax a bit," said Rose.

"I know. I feel like I could use a couple more hours of sleep, too," Mitzi said as she rubbed her eyes awake. "I think he's just excited."

"Not to mention, he didn't stay up chattin' half the night like we did." Rose chuckled and threw her pillow at Mitzi where it landed straight on her face. Mitzi laughed and chucked it back at her, missing by a mile.

"Hope you can read a map better than you can throw a pillow," Rose teased.

"I'm just hoping my dad will let us study that map in his office without asking too many questions, you know?" Mitzi looked concerned.

The girls quickly got dressed and brushed their teeth and raced to the kitchen to meet Finn and grab a quick bite. As they entered the kitchen, Finn looked up from his bowl of cereal and Mitzi's dad sipped from a cup of coffee as he scrolled through his phone.

"Good morning, ladies," he said without taking his eyes off his screen.

"Morning!" the girls replied in unison.

"Finn tells me that you want to study the property map in my office?" He looked up at them.

"Yep. Is that alright with you, Dad?" Mitzi held her breath.

"I guess so," her dad answered. "Just please don't touch anything in there or go snooping around. Plus, you are going to have to look quickly. I have a morning meeting that starts in about a half hour."

"No problem, Dad." Mitzi sat in silence for a moment. "You never have a morning meeting…you working on some big case, Dad?"

"Well, not that it's any of your business, but yes. This new case is more important than most that

I've had in a while. It's not the usual 'open and shut' case I normally get around here. I may be putting in some extra hours for a while until we get it resolved." He looked worried and worn out.

Mitzi wondered if this case had anything to do with the conversation they overheard up in the attic about the missing person named Martin. She wanted to ask but couldn't without throwing herself and friends under the bus for eavesdropping.

Mitzi and Rose shared an English muffin as Finn finished his cereal, and then the three made their way to the office. The map looked old and was the color of iced tea. The writing on it was fancy and looked like it was made by hand. The bottom right corner edge had a key and the date 1919 and the words 'Clark Estate Plan'.

The map was large and took up most of the wall opposite the window. It showed the house and driveway on the lower right quarter. Up in the top left corner was a small rectangle marked 'B.C, and the three agreed that it must be the cabin.

Between the house and the cabin was the tree line. The cabin looked to be set in a clearing in the middle of a small forest. Behind the cabin was a small stream that ran across the top of the map.

"Looks like we need to walk through a bit of forest to get to the spot of the old cabin." Mitzi pointed to the trees on the map.

"Well, I hope you got bug spray. I can't stand bugs!" Rose complained.

"I don't think that bugs will be our biggest problem," Finn said. "I have a feeling that there may not exactly be a path back there. I bet it's all overgrown. This may be quite a pain in the butt, you know."

"Let's just go and check it out." Mitzi sighed. "I'll get the clippers out of the shed in case we need them to clear a path. I'll grab us some drinks and snacks, too."

"Don't forget the bug spray!!!" Rose ordered.

"I won't forget the bug spray!" Mitzi said a bit impatiently.

Chapter Eight

The sky was cloudy as the three set off on their morning trek to find the old site. They walked in silence toward the tree line for several minutes. Mitzi was deep in thought and her mind raced. *This might just be a big waste of time. There is probably nothing even back there. I mean, what would be back there anyway? Maybe another old stamp? That would be cool, but what else could be there? I guess it's kind of cool to check out where my grandfather used to play as a kid, but I have a feeling this is going to be disappointing.*

"My feet hurt already." Rose's complaint interrupted the silence.

"Oh, get a grip," Finn teased. "I think you can make it." He laughed to himself and pushed his glasses up his nose. "Besides, we will be at *the fun* part in a couple minutes." He pointed to the tree line ahead, and Rose let out a small groan.

"I don't think it will be that bad, Rose." Mitzi smiled. "We can walk along the tree line to try to find the clearest way through."

Finn stopped in his tracks and thrust his arm into the air and stood like a cartoon superhero about to take off flying. "We shall find the path of least resistance!!!" Finn shouted in his deepest voice, and then laughed as he resumed his walking.

"You're *such* a dork," Rose teased.

Finn blew a raspberry in her direction. "Maybe we will get lucky and spot a game trail."

Finn tripped on a rock and almost fell.

"Nice moves, Superman…but what the heck is a game trail, anyway?" Rose asked.

Finn raised his eyebrows and, with a smarty-pants look on his face, said, "A game trail is like a path made in the woods or tall thick grasses by animals that live and travel through the area on a regular basis... you know, like dear ... fox ... bears ... rabbits ... that kind of thing." He looked proud of himself. "I think it's pretty sweet how they make their own little roadways that they use again and again."

"In that case, let's split up and see if we can find the best-looking path that's headed that way." Mitzi pointed toward the left and the three started walking apart and carefully peering into the forest.

In very little time at all, Rose shouted out, "This looks like a decent path! Come check it out!"

Mitzi grinned from ear to ear when she caught up to Rose

"Wow! That is an excellent path. I think that looks like an old man-made trail. Fantastic!" Finn gave a thumbs up to Rose, who rolled her eyes at his cheesy gesture.

The path was mostly gravel and dirt, with spikes of grasses that had pushed up over the years. It was a couple feet wide and looked as though it had been used a lot in the past.

"You know," said Rose, "this cabin we're looking for was a builder's cabin, right?"

"Yeah, so?" Finn looked at her curiously.

"So… the builders needed a path to the build site. Right?" Rose raised her hands and shrugged.

"You're right!" Mitzi looked excited. "This must be an old roadway from when the builders had to go back and forth every day!"

"One might even say…" Finn paused, "it was a builders GAME trail…" Finn chuckled at his own joke.

"Oh, Finn. Sometimes, I just don't know about your sense of humor," Rose picked.

"Sometimes I don't know about your face." Finn cut back.

"Oh, give it a rest, you two!" Mitzi took a deep breath. "We have this great looking path here. What do you both say we get on it?"

The three started in silence down the path. "We should keep a lookout for any clues," Mitzi said softly.

"What kind of clues would we be looking for here?" Rose asked.

Mitzi considered her reply for a minute. "I'm not really sure, exactly… but it was in the tree line that I first found the stamp, right?"

"I have an idea." Finn said. "Why don't I look in the trees and brush to the left...Rose to the right...and Mitzi, you scan the path. That way we don't miss anything."

"That sounds like a good plan," Rose agreed.

The trio moved slowly along the path, each scanning their assigned area for clues. As Finn and Rose walked, they bickered about the latest episode of their favorite YouTuber, *Split Nugget.* Mitzi was careful to scan her area so as not to miss a single inch. After about fifteen minutes, the path started to widen, and Mitzi looked up from her scanning to see they had arrived at a large clearing.

"I think we are here!" Mitzi smiled, and with a buzz of excitement, the three took off in a run.

The clearing was thick with weeds and tall grasses. It had obviously been neglected for a long time. It wasn't hard to find the spot of the old cabin, though, because some of the exterior wall was still jotting out of the ground, black and rotted from fire and time. The trio walked the perimeter of the remains, inside and out, and found nothing but dirt, rocks, and disappointment.

"There's gotta be something here," Mitzi complained, and slapped her hands to her legs in frustration.

Finn looked up at her from the rocks he was examining and said, "If there is anything here, I don't think it's in this mess. I imagine this place was searched and emptied before they burned it to the ground."

"I gotta agree with Finny on this one, Mitz," Rose added.

"Okay. That's fair. But if you were to hide something important, where would you hide it out here?" Mitzi started pacing the cabin grounds.

"Hmmmm… If I wanted to hide something … I might bury it … or find a hollowed-out tree … or under stones … something like that."

She stopped pacing and turned toward her friends. "Rose, why don't you check the trees for any hollow spots that something could be tucked in…and you, Finn, check along the stream for any signs of a hiding place." She crinkled her nose with determination. "I will walk through the grasses from the trail back to the stream in a grid pattern and see if I can find anything. We probably won't find anything but since we are here, we should at least look thoroughly."

"I guess it won't hurt to check everything out," agreed Rose.

"Sounds good to me, too." Finn dropped the rock he was examining and dusted his hands. "We better make quick work of it, though." He pointed up at the sky, which was becoming darker by the minute. "I think we're about to get rained out, and by the look of that sky, we may get some thunder and lightning, too."

"Then let's do this now. Holler out if you find anything!" Mitzi yelled as the three all headed out in different directions.

Mitzi rubbed her eyes after several minutes of searching in the tall grasses. She kept hoping one of her friends would shout out a discovery. Instead, she heard only the stream trickling by and a bird chirping here and there.

She was startled by a sudden drop of rain hitting her face. She reached her hand to her cheek to wipe away the drip as the sky quickly opened up into a downpour.

"Oh my gosh!" Rose yelled as she ran under a giant oak tree for cover.

"Hey! Make room under there!" Finn raised his arms over his head in an unsuccessful attempt to keep somewhat dry. Mitzi just stood in the grass. She lifted her head to the sky and closed her eyes. She loved the feel of the cold rain on her face.

"I guess we need to put our search on hold!" she yelled to her friends through the loud downpour.

"You think?" Rose said with a sarcastic expression as she squeezed water out of her braids.

"We are already soaked." Mitzi shrugged. "We might as well head back and get dry before my mom sends a search party out for us."

"Alright. But … last one there is a rotten egg!" Rose pushed Finn back toward the tree trunk as she took off running toward the house.

"Ha!" Mitzi giggled and turned to run after her.

"Oh man! I don't want to race." Finn pushed his water speckled glasses up his nose and jogged halfheartedly behind them. "I hate running," Mitzi heard him whine under his breath.

Chapter Nine

The 'Rotten Egg' was Finn. Rose was the first to reach the front door, and the three stood catching their breaths as they dripped puddles of water onto the porch. Mitzi pushed open the door and yelled out for her mother to get them some towels.

"My word, Mitzo! You guys are soaked to the bone!" She handed each of them a towel and chuckled to herself. "I had a feeling the three of you would get stuck out in the rain. Come on down to the kitchen and I'll fix you some cocoa so you can dry off a bit before I bring you two kids home."

The trio sat around the kitchen table as Mitzi's mom delivered steaming mugs of cocoa.

"We can head out as soon as Dad is done with his business. One of his associates blocked my car in, so we will just go when he goes...that Marty!" Deb shook her head. "I told him just last week not to park like that!"

The three looked up quickly at the sound of the name Marty. Marty was the name of the man that had disappeared.

"Now finish up that cocoa, you two … I think I hear them wrapping up."

All three kids strained to hear the conversation coming from down the hall.

Mitzi just caught bits and pieces.

"Just glad you are safe…"

"Stick to protocol…"

"Wish you would just trust me…"

She didn't know what any of it meant. She just knew it was important. It all felt connected somehow. She was determined to get to the bottom of it.

Finn and Rose stood to go, and Mitzi said, "We will talk later, guys. I'm going to keep working."

"Let us know if you turn up anything new," Finn whispered.

***

Instead of getting into dry clothes right away, Mitzi took a detour to the attic to see if she could hear anything from the floor grate that might explain Marty's recent disappearance and reappearance.

As she kneeled close to the vent, she could hear what sounded like her father on the phone with someone. "Yes…yes, of course not. I'm not stupid. He definitely didn't seem like himself at all. Yes, I used salt, silver, sage, and even birch ash. He had no reaction … Deb is trailing him now. Let's just stick to article 14. We will talk soon."

And then it was quiet.

Mitzi was trying hard to sort out this new information in her mind. *So, Marty returned from who-knows-where and is acting strangely. Hmm. What's with the salt and silver? Spices and ash? I am so confused! Why is MOM trailing him? What is my family a part of?*

Mitzi shook her head in confusion as a queasy feeling grew in her stomach. She was starting to realize that her father was most likely not a lawyer after all.

Mitzi snuck back down to her bedroom and changed into some jeans and a dry shirt. She plopped down on her bed and stared at the ceiling. "What am I missing?" she said out loud to no-one. "Where haven't I looked?"

"I know!"

She sat up and felt a small rush of excitement. *I can check out the books on the shelves and see if there are any more hints there!* Mitzi sprung off her bed and zoomed down to the living room.

She didn't really know what she was looking for, so she gently pulled at each book, thinking she might get lucky and uncover some kind of secret passageway or something. She stood on a stool to reach the top three shelves, and didn't find anything other than a lot of dust. *Okay, Mitzi … think.* One by one, she read the titles out loud softly to herself, hoping that something odd would stand out.

The top three shelves were filled with old law books. The next shelf was a mix of historical non-fiction and dictionaries, and some classic Fiction like 'Moby Dick' and 'To Kill a Mockingbird'. The next shelf down was more Fiction, but two books caught her eye. One was titled 'The Art of Throwing Knives' and the other 'Into the Secret Night'.

She flipped through the pages and, although she found their presence intriguing, they seemed to be *just* books. Once she was finished looking through the books on the whole shelf to the left of the fireplace, she dusted off her hands on her jeans and sat down on the chair to take a break.

She heard the door creek open. She turned toward the door as her father stepped in. "Whatcha doing in here, kiddo? Your friends went home?"

Mitzi smiled at her dad and nodded. "I was just looking for something to read," she lied. "Any suggestions?"

"Oh. Good!" He scratched his chin. "I always liked reading the Narnia books..." He pointed to the right. "Mom likes that one about the wizard school kid."

"Yeah. Maybe I'll check out one of those." But then Mitzi got an idea. "Did my great grandfather have a favorite book?"

"Well, as a matter of fact, he did!" Her dad smiled. "My father told me that he was never seen without his copy of 'Moby Dick' tucked under his arm. I still don't get what your new fascination is with him, though…"

"I just think it's kind of cool to learn about him, is all…" Mitzi tried to appear disinterested, but she was about to burst with excitement.

"Anyway," her dad sighed, "I just wanted to let you know that I'm headed up for a quick nap…in case you wondered where I went."

"You alright, Dad?" Mitzi never saw her dad look so worn out and was a bit concerned for him. He wasn't someone who took naps.

"Yes! No cause for alarm, my sweet girl. Just a lot of stuff going on with work and I'm just tired out is all." He smiled as he left the room.

As quickly as he left, Mitzi rushed to the shelf and pulled out the leather-bound copy of 'Moby Dick'. It was faded brown, and leather bound with gold, fancy lettering. Her heart stopped as she turned open the cover and revealed an inscription on the very first page. Written in black fancy handwriting was, *Frederick Clark.* But what was even more interesting to Mitzi was what was written in very small letters underneath. It simply said, *J1.*

"No way!" Mitzi exclaimed in disbelief.

I can't believe I found another clue. But what do they mean? I need to call Finn and Rose… We gotta figure this out. Can they be a combination to a safe? Maybe a lock?

As quietly as she could, Mitzi raced to her phone and called Finn and Rose on a three-way call.

"You guys are never going to believe this." Mitzi could hardly contain her excitement.

"Did you figure it out?" Rose asked.

"Did you find another clue?" Finn questioned.

"Yes! I mean, no! I mean, no, I didn't figure it out, but yes, I found another clue!" Mitzi felt proud of herself.

"Well, spit it out, Mitzi!" Rose giggled. "Whatcha find?"

Mitzi explained to them about searching through the books and then how her dad came in and told her about 'Moby Dick'.

"...and when I opened to the first page, it was right there in plain sight!" Mitzi finished.

"What was the clue? What did it say?" Finn sounded like he was about to burst with anticipation.

Mitzi cleared her throat. "It had my great grandfather's name, written in his fancy letters, and underneath that, is the letter J and the number 1!"

"Holy Crap!" Finn exclaimed.

"This is seriously crazy, Mitzi. I mean, at first, I kinda thought this mystery was a waste of time if I'm being real…but even I can't deny it now!" Rose admitted.

"Now we just need to figure out what this means." Mitzi sounded discouraged.

"Actually," Finn said, "I have a new theory about our clues."

"Do tell," Mitzi said

"So, I was thinking…and I don't know why I didn't think of it before…but when I got home, my brothers were playing the game *Battleship* and it totally came to me!"

"What? A game, Finn? Seriously?" Rose sounded annoyed.

"Just hear me out, Rose." Finn cleared his throat. "In the game, you arrange different sized boats on a grid that stays hidden from the other player. They have to try to guess where you put your boats by calling out possible coordinates, like B1 or C7. The letters are the rows, and the numbers are the columns. Then it hit me like a bolt of dang lightning! Maybe, our G5, is a coordinate and we need to look again at…"

"THE MAP!" Mitzi interrupted.

"Yes, the map!" Finn finished.

"I don't remember seeing any letters or numbers on that thing." Rose sounded skeptical. "But then again, we weren't really looking for any either."

"Any chance you can get back in there and check again?" Finn asked.

"My dad is taking a nap right now, but I will ask him when he gets up," Mitzi said.

"OR…you can sneak in there and look right now," Rose said in a sing-song way.

"Come on, Rose. You know I can't…"

"It really wouldn't take that long," Finn interrupted.

"He would never even know you were in there," Rose added.

There was a long pause as Mitzi considered the risks of getting caught.

Mitzi let out a big sigh. "Okay. I'll do it. After all, he is taking a nap and I can get in and out of there in about one-minute flat."

"OMG!" Rose blurted.

"Good luck, Mitzi," Finn said. "Call us as soon as you're done." He hung up.

"Yeah, don't get caught...bye!" Rose hung up, too.

Mitzi took a deep breath and held it. She didn't like to break the rules. On the other hand, she didn't want to wait and ask permission either. Her dad already seemed suspicious, and asking to look at the map again would definitely add to it. It was a small crime.

Mitzi exhaled and started toward the office as she whispered under her breath, "Guess it's now or never."

CHAPTER TEN

She stood at the office door and listened for several seconds for any signs that her dad was no longer napping. Satisfied he was still resting, she opened the door and quickly went to study the map again. She saw them right away. The small handwritten letters along the right and left edges and the numbers lightly written along the top and bottom of the map.

I can't believe we didn't notice them before! I guess we were just too focused on finding the cabin...

Starting at the bottom left corner of the map, she followed the letters

Up from 'A' until she stopped at the letter 'J'. She held her left pointer finger on the 'J' and then started back at the corner and moved her right pointer finger to the number '1' along the bottom. Then she moved her right finger straight up the map and her left finger over to meet the spot where they would connect. The spot was equally between the top left corner of the old builder's cabin and a sharp bend in the stream.

"I wonder if something is buried there?" she whispered out loud.

She repeated the process to find 'G' and '5', and a rush of excitement surged through her as her fingers settled on the exact spot on the map that she had found the silver stamp sticking out of the dirt at the tree line.

If G5 was the location of the stamp, then J1 has to be significant. I just know it!

Mitzi tiptoed out of the office and back to the front hall, considering carefully how to proceed with her next plan.

I will leave a note…grab a shovel out of the shed, and head back out to the clearing at the cabin.

She left a note in the kitchen for her mother when she returned from town, which should have really been any time. It was still raining, so she got her old blue raincoat and rubber boots from the coat closet. She opened the front door as quietly as she could so as not to wake her father and stepped out into the late afternoon rain. She made her way around the side of the house to the small shed that housed the gardening tools and found a big, old, pointed shovel in the corner behind the rakes and made her way toward the clearing.

The walk didn't seem to take that long this time. Perhaps that was because Mitzi was so excited that her pace was quick, and that this time, she knew exactly where to go. When she arrived at the clearing, she went straight to the remains of the old cabin and found the back-left corner of the foundation. She looked over at the small river and searched for the sharp turn on the bank.

"There!" she shouted and pointed at the place along the bank.

I can count how many steps it is between this corner and that spot on the bank of the river. Then, halfway back should be the spot.

As she stepped, trying hard to keep each step the same size, she counted out loud. "...forty-seven...forty-eight..."

She stopped as she noticed a small pile of round rocks stacked together just a bit off to the right of where she was standing. She also noticed that she was about halfway to the river. *I bet that is it! I'm gonna keep going, though... just to be sure.*

When she reached the spot on the bank, she finished her count with, "One hundred and three."

That rock pile was at 48! That's about halfway!

She knelt beside the pile of rocks. Each was about the size of grapefruit. There was grass and mud between them from many seasons and they were stuck together. She pulled and scraped at them with her fingers; they were slippery from the rain. One by one, she piled them neatly to the side, planning on returning them exactly as she found them when she was finished searching. After moving the seventh and final rock, she stood with her shovel, ready to dig.

The ground was soft from all the rain. It wasn't easy work, though, as the rain made each pile of shoveled mud heavy, too. Mitzi pushed the shovel into the ground, hoping to hear and feel it hit something. A few times, she struck something hard and felt excitement rush through her only to discover that she had just hit a rock.

She dug and dug. The hole was getting pretty deep. Mitzi thought it looked about two feet deep and about a foot around. *Maybe I just missed it on the side? Guess I will need to make the hole wider. When I found the stamp, it was poking out of the surface, so it wasn't buried that deep.*

Mitzi started digging around the sides of the hole, making it wider. When she plunged the shovel into the ground the fifth time, it stopped with a sudden, strange, and hollow THUD! She quickly shoveled out a few more scoops of dirt around the top of what seemed to be a fairly large object. Bits of dark brown became visible through the mud. She didn't want to hurt the buried object with the shovel, so she sat on the soggy ground to finish digging it out by hand.

As she pulled at the handfuls of mud, she could tell the object was a box made of wood. It was about the size of a laptop. She cleared one end of the box and gripped it as firmly as she could and pulled. It made a slurping suction sound as it pulled free from the ground.

Mitzi used the sleeve of her raincoat to wipe off as much of the mud from the box as she could. She was worried that the rain might ruin whatever was inside but didn't want to wait to open it. She remembered the big oak had provided pretty good rain cover earlier. With her mysterious treasure box tucked under her arm, Mitzi ran to the giant tree and sat with her back against the trunk and the box resting on her lap.

Although she still felt a few drops of rain here and there, dropping off the leaves, the tree did seem to provide some protection from the rain.

Examining the box on her lap, she noticed it was quite a plain box with a simple hook and latch clasp on one side. She moved her thumb along the clasp to pop open the latch. It was a bit stiff, but Mitzi managed to pry it open fairly quickly.

She held her breath as she lifted the lid, and her eyes widened at the sight of a black leather-bound book. About halfway down the cover, the book was held shut with a leather strap and buckle but there were no words or anything else printed on the cover.

Mitzi wiped her hands up and down her wet jeans to clean off the dirt as best as she could before handling the book. She slowly removed the book and examined it on every side. It was plain all around. As carefully as she could, she unbuckled the strap and pulled back the front cover.

Written in the familiar lettering of F.C. Clark, Mitzi read the title scrolled across the first page, "The American Chapter guidebook of the Society for Hiding Undesirable Truths."

What the heck? She scratched her head and flipped through the book. The first few pages were lists of membership guidelines followed by an oath of secrecy. *Oh my goodness. Is this some kind of secret society?* As she turned the pages, a mixture of wonder, curiosity, and terror washed through her body.

The next section of the book was 'Supernatural Objects and Their Proper Care or Disposal'. There were sketches of objects on the left of the page, and notes on the right like... *The box of Doom: Cannot be destroyed, must be kept under chains. Opening brings 30 days of black rain and plague. And...*

Chalice of permanent sleep: Can only be destroyed by Star magic, must be hidden until appropriate time. One sip from chalice brings permanent sleep.

Mitzi couldn't believe what she was seeing. The guidebook had dozens and dozens of objects listed. *Is this just a made-up story? Was this a game or the real thing?*

The next section of the guidebook was designated to 'Helpful Tools and Weapons of the Hunt'. It listed things like, arrows dipped in crushed garnet stone to kill a Siren…

What the heck is a siren?

And tips like, *if a wooden stake is not available, try dipping your blade in hot wax and then turning it in sawdust. This will deliver wood to the heart of the vampire, rendering it dead.*

Mitzi looked off into the distance. Her head was spinning with thoughts and questions.

This must just be some kind of club they had or something. There are no such things as supernatural beings, right? I mean, if these things were real, the whole world would know about it. They would have proof or something. This seems like old-school cosplay or something. But it seems so real…so official…important. What if it is real? What if this is something I'm not supposed to see?

The last section of the book was perhaps the most interesting. It was a section on 'Creatures and Beings of a Non-Human Nature'.

Her eyes widened as she read the heading again. With feelings of disbelief mixed with curiosity, she turned page after page. Each of the pages had a creature name at the top with a sketch of it underneath. Under the sketches, on the right, was a column titled, 'Strengths' and on the left, 'Weaknesses'.

She had heard of some of the creatures before, like vampires, werewolves, bigfoot, ghosts, demons, goblins, and witches. All of which she had believed to be fictional creatures and folklore. Some of the creatures, however, were completely new to her.

The Eastern Baltovey was one example. The sketch looked like a regular man but with a face like a rodent. Its eyes looked human enough, but its nose was long and slopped down to its protruding sharp front teeth. It had bushy, dark eyebrows and a wiry, bristly looking beard. The strengths were listed as, 'can shrink or grow at will' and 'collects secrets to trade with Demons'. The weaknesses listed were, 'Water is lethal' and 'Cats'.

What in the heck? This thing is some kind of Rat-man?

And DEMONS? This HAS to be made-up... Right? Mitzi knew she had to get the book home and hidden. She needed help deciphering the crazy thing, and Rose and Finn were just a phone call away. She closed the book and held it tightly in her arms, flabbergasted with the choices before her.

I mean, if these things are real, it would change everything. I don't even know what to do with this information. Should I show it to Dad?

She squeezed the book closer to her chest, unsure of her next steps.

Mitzi stood and put the book back in the box, hugging it tightly to her body as she started toward home. When she got close to the house, she tucked the box under her raincoat and cradled it under her arm hoping she could sneak it up to her bedroom, unnoticed.

Lucky for her, when she arrived, the house was still and quiet. She figured her dad was still sleeping but, *Mom should have been back by now...odd*. She shook her head and returned her thoughts to the task at hand.

Mitzi tip-toed up the stairs as quickly as she could. It was cold and she was sick of her skin feeling so wet. After tossing her rain-soaked clothes into the laundry, she was happy to wrestle on a pair of comfy sweatpants and an old t-shirt. Curled up under a blanket with the box on her lap and the house phone clasped in her hands, she was ready to call for back-up.

CHAPTER ELEVEN

Finn and Rose were shocked to hear about the discovery of such a strange and curious book. After going back and forth on theories for about an hour, the three concluded that the book was most probably something that was created as part of a game. It *must* have been a fantasy story game like Dungeons and Dragons.

Although Mitzi believed that was the most logical explanation, something was pulling inside her mind, not letting her let go of the fact that there may have been a world that she had never known about...

Part of her wanted the book to be true even though if it were true, it would be terrifying.

Her stomach growled in hunger, so she decided she would go and have some dinner and then turn in early for the night.

Downstairs, the house was quiet and dark. She looked out the front window and was surprised that her mother still had not returned home. She knocked softly on her father's office door. "Hey Dad?" she asked softly.

"Come in, Mitzo," he answered.

She opened the door just enough to poke her head in. Her dad still looked tired, and was bent over paperwork that was scrambled all over his desk. "Do you know that Mom isn't back yet?" Mitzi cocked her head to the side.

"Umm... yeah... I... umm..." Her father was distracted and scattered. "She called and I umm... I am going to meet her in town for a last-minute meeting, so..." His voice trailed off.

"Oh!" Mitzi was thrown off guard. Something seemed off.

I think Dad looks worried…not tired. It feels like something is going on here that he's not telling me.

"Can I at least make you some dinner before you head out?" she offered.

"I'll grab something while I am out, honey, but thank you." He stood and grabbed a black duffle bag from under his desk and slung it on his shoulder. "In fact, I need to head out now…" His voice trailed off again, and he kissed Mitzi on the top of her head as he stepped past her toward the door. "See you in a bit…shouldn't be too long…" And then he was gone.

Mitzi stood in the dark hallway, feeling bewildered by the recent events. *What the heck is going on here? First, Mom doesn't come home after dropping off my friends in town like four hours ago … and now, suddenly, Dad is acting weird and nervous and says they have some meeting in town… I don't think he is telling me the truth.*

What if Mom went missing like that Martin dude?

Mitzi felt as though her head would explode. She was letting her imagination run wild and knew she needed to calm down. She took in a deep breath, held it for a few seconds, then let it out slowly to relax herself. *There has got to be a rational explanation for all of this.* As if on cue, her stomach growled a low groan, reminding Mitzi that she was hungry, so she turned to the kitchen to make a sandwich.

***

It was about an hour later when she heard the grumblings of two cars pulling up to the house. Mitzi peered out the window, relieved to see both of her parents return.

See, Mitzi, you were worried for nothing! Now I can get some sleep and dig into this mystery more in the morning.

But she couldn't sleep. She tossed and turned in bed for what felt like hours. Her mind raced through thought after thought as the creatures in the book flashed in her mind's eye. It was after midnight when she sat up and turned on her table lamp. She grabbed the book from under her bed and studied its pages again.

Mitzi read the membership guidelines section and found it to be fairly generic and a bit boring. The guidelines were things like... *all information pertaining to the society must be kept secret and private* ... and ... *All new members must be unanimously selected by the Order Elders...*

Mitzi rubbed her eyes. She was starting to feel a bit sleepy as she moved onto reading the *Oath of Secrecy...*

I, (New Member's name), do solemnly swear to keep the Secrets of The Society for Hiding Undesirable Truths. I will protect these secrets with everything I have, up to and including, my life. I will honor the society code and protect our members and our secrets until the day I die.

Mitzi read the oath several times. She wanted to believe that the book was a child's game, but each time she read the words, she couldn't help but think they were real … that these monsters and magical things did, in fact, exist. Without realizing it, she drifted off into a dreamless sleep with the book still in her hands.

Chapter Twelve

The next day, Mitzi felt groggy and worn out from staying up so late the night before. She stashed the book back under her bed and went to the kitchen for a bite to eat. She expected to see her mother in her usual morning spot but was instead surprised to find the house empty and quiet. After a quick bowl of cereal, Mitzi decided to look for her mom to ask her about her short disappearance the night before. As she turned into the living room, she noticed her mother was standing at the fireplace and staring at the books.

"Good morning, Ma!" Mitzi greeted.

"OH!" Deb was startled. "Good morning, dear child. What are your plans for the day?"

Something seemed off to Mitzi. First of all, her mother never called her 'dear child' and secondly, her voice sounded funny…like sing-songy and almost fake. She decided she must have been imagining things and should just answer.

"I'm not really sure," Mitzi said as she realized she wasn't sure what to do next, as far as the book and the mystery were concerned.

"You must play outside today." Her mother flashed a toothy, overly dramatic grin at Mitzi. "Please do not return until lunch time. I have important things to do and cannot have you underfoot today." Her smile dropped in a flash, and she pointed at the door for Mitzi to leave.

"Okay then…" Mitzi was in shock. "I'll just grab some stuff from my room and head outside then."

"Yes, dear. You do that. Bye," said her mother's robotic voice as she turned back to study the books on the shelves.

Mitzi wanted to ask her what she was looking for, or where she had been last night, but she knew it wasn't the right time. Something super bazaar was going on and Mitzi had no idea what to do about it. *Maybe I should talk to Dad...Yes! He will tell me what's up with Mom.* But as Mitzi approached his office door, her confusion grew at the sight of a sticky note that simply said, *Back Later, Dad.*

Mitzi paced back and forth in her room, trying hard to come up with a plan on what to do next. She couldn't figure out why her mother was acting so strangely or where her dad was. She didn't know what to do about the book, or even the stamp. She felt like crying. Everything felt wrong. All of a sudden, an idea struck her. She sat on the edge of her bed with her phone and called Rose.

"Hey, Rose. I gotta be quick here…so listen carefully," she whispered into the phone.

"Okay, Mitz. You alright? Why are you so quiet?" Rose sounded concerned.

"Yes, yes, I'm fine. I will explain later. I need you to do something for me…" Mitzi said.

"What do you need?" Rose asked.

"I need you to meet me at the library…see if you can bring Finny." Mitzi sounded stressed.

"That's easy, no problem. But will you first tell me what is going on here?" Rose sounded a bit annoyed.

"I promise I will fill you in as soon as I get there. First, I need to convince my mom to bring me to town. See you soon!" And she hung up the phone.

Mitzi stuffed the stamp, the book, her phone, and her notebook into her old school backpack and took a deep breath. "Well…here goes nothing!" Her voice sounded steady and strong despite the bundle of nervous butterflies growing larger in her gut by the second.

As she turned to face her mother in the living room again, she was surprised to see her still looking at the books. With her back still toward Mitzi, her mother spoke in a low voice. "I thought I told you to go outside for the day?"

Slightly scared at the tone of her mother's voice, Mitzi struggled to find enough bravery to continue her plan. She cleared her throat and said, "Yes, Mom. Erm … sorry but … Rose called and wants to meet at the library for arts and crafts and then her mom says that me and Finny can stay for dinner. So, I was wondering if you could drive…"

"Can't you see that I am busy here?!" her mother snapped at her without looking up from the books.

Mitzi's heart was pounding in her chest as she pushed on forward. "I just thought it may be better for you if I was out of your hair all day, instead of only until lunchtime. Sorry to have bothered you." Mitzi turned to leave.

"Wait! My dear, I shall take you. That would be better, I think." Her mother's voice was sing-songy and robotic again.

Yes. My plan is working! Mitzi smiled to herself and let herself relax a bit. *Hopefully, Finn and Rose can help me figure out what the heck to do next.*

CHAPTER THIRTEEN

"Girl, you are looking a bit pale," Rose said as the trio sat down in a quiet corner of the town library. "You okay?" Mitzi scrambled through her bag and pulled out the black leather book and sat it on the table before them.

"I am actually kind of freaking out a bit, guys." She looked back and forth between her friends' curious faces. "I mean, I think this book is REAL."

"What?" Finn sounded unconvinced. "Seriously, Mitzi? How can it be real? Creatures and ghosts and crap like that? I don't think so."

Rose sighed. "I'm with the Finster on this one. I just don't buy it, and I'm surprised that you do."

Mitzi looked serious. "Normally, I wouldn't buy into anything like this at all. *But* the pieces are all fitting together and the puzzle is taking shape. Think about it, you guys…" She was pleading with her friends, "First, we find the stamp and the clues that lead to this book, just as we overhear my dad talking about a missing person who reappears and is acting strangely….and then…my mom disappears for a few hours and now she is acting super bizarre! It's gotta be all connected!"

Rose and Finn sat quietly for a second, surprised by how upset Mitzi was. Rose quietly asked, "Hey Mitz? Why don't you just talk to your dad about all of this now? I think it's time."

Mitzi looked at her friend as her eyes filled with tears. "Because I don't know where he is. He is missing now, too."

Finn and Rose both sat back in their chairs, shocked by the news.

After sitting in silence for a bit, Finn leaned in. "I guess we had better study these creatures then...try to figure out what we may be dealing with here."

Rose nodded in agreement.

"Also," Mitzi tapped her forehead with her pointer finger, "I need to remember that name we overheard in the attic ... the investigation… I have a feeling that has something to do with all of this somehow. My dad seemed to think so anyway when Martin went missing… Was it Hanson? Or Harrison? I really wish that I wrote it down."

"HALBERT!" Finn practically yelled as several "shhhhs" came from other library patrons.

"Yes, that's it!" Mitzi looked hopeful. "I will start looking for any info on the Halbert name, and you two can look through the book and see what you can come up with."

"Let's do this," Rose said, and the three started their quiet investigations.

As Rose and Finn poured over the guidebook, Mitzi searched the internet for any information that she could find on the name Halbert. She searched a popular website that people used for researching census data and family tree information that she had heard about on TV. She quickly learned that the name Halbert was of English origin and it means a person that makes weapons.

By the year 1930, there were about seventeen Halbert families living in New York, including one family listed in Hadford. *Okay, so there is a family in town with that name...but is there any news on that family?* She searched phrases like 'Hadford Halbert Crime' and 'Halbert Family Hadford' and wasn't able to find out anything at all. The only thing that she was able to find was an address: 122 County Road 6.

She plugged the address into Google earth and was bummed to see it was pretty far outside of town ... definitely not somewhere they could walk. *Maybe this is a dead-end, she thought. I mean, what am I going to do? Walk up to the front door and knock and say, 'Hello there...by the way, do you have my dad?' Ugh. Maybe Finn and Rose got somewhere with the guidebook.*

As Mitzi walked toward the table, Finn was feverishly writing notes as Rose was flipping through the pages.

"This is some seriously crazy business right here," Rose mumbled without looking up from the page she was on.

Finn pushed his glasses up his nose and looked up at Mitzi. "I think we have narrowed it down to a few possibilities ... a few crazy possibilities.

Well, it's more like we have made a list of all the creatures in the book ... and then we crossed them out if there is something that excludes them from being likely. For example..." Finn scratched his head. "We are not likely dealing with a vampire because Martin and your mother both came back. A vampire would have just killed them for sure. We eliminated ghosts because this whole situation doesn't fit the profile of a ghost haunting at all, and so on... You see?" Finn cocked his head to the side and looked Mitzi in the eye.

"So, then what creature *does* fit, Finn?" Mitzi asked.

"You gotta understand, this isn't exactly a science but based on everything we do know, Rose and I have narrowed it down to a few possibilities. The first one is a creature called a Cibusannus, which, according to the guidebook, is Latin for Eating Years.

They are human-like immortals that somehow steal time out of a person's life and that is how they live forever. The guidebook says the only way to recognize them is that they have slits like fish gills behind their ears, but cover them up when they are in public. They also move every few years so that people don't notice that they never age."

Mitzi felt sick in her stomach and her mind was racing in a million directions. *Maybe my mother's behavior was a side effect of having years of her life taken from her? But if it was a Cibusannus that took them, why now? Why all at once? I don't think this is the right creature....*

"That's definitely interesting. What else do you got?" Mitzi looked hopefully at her friends.

Rose cleared her throat. "You aren't gonna like the next one." She paused and looked at Mitzi, who motioned with her hands for Rose to continue. "It may be a Demon. Demons take over the body of their target and stay as long as they need to. The bad news is when a demon leaves the host, most of the time the host will die… It's probably not a demon, Mitzi. I think because…"

Mitzi interrupted, "What do you mean by most of the time?"

Rose turned a few pages into the guidebook and read out loud. "The host can be saved during a demon exodus if they swallow the serum of 'sanare illustris' or 'healing light' before the demon is expelled." Rose put the book down as she added, "It also says that demons prefer the night and often sleep during the day, and both your mom and Martin were awake in the day so that's good, right?" Rose shrugged.

"I just hope that isn't why my dad had to take a nap yesterday." Mitzi was worried.

"Well, if it makes you feel any better, the guidebook says that the society has the serum of Sanare illustris in its inventory … wherever that is..." Finn added.

Mitzi was starting to get a headache. "I hope we never need to find it. What other creatures are possibilities?"

"Mitzi, I don't think we are going about this the right way," Finn blurted out.

"What do you mean, Finn?" Mitzi was intrigued.

"It just seems like we can spin around and round here with guesswork. But then what? What's the point here?" he finished.

"What do I do then? I gotta do something!" Mitzi raised her voice, and a few more shushes flooded the library. "Sorry!" she murmured and took a deep breath.

"Is there someone we could go to? Maybe my dad can help?" Rose offered. "He is the sheriff after all."

"Thanks, Rose, but I don't think... Wait! I know! Maybe Mr. Moore can help us!" Mitzi said in an excited whisper. For the first time all day, a grin washed over Mitzi's face. "He will know what to do."

Chapter Fourteen

Rose convinced her mother to drive the three kids out to Mr. Moore's house with a story that they planned to surprise the old man by doing yard work for him. When the trio got out of the car, Mr. Moore was sitting on his porch rocking in an old wooden rocker, sipping what looked like iced tea. A toothless grin flashed across his face at his unexpected visitors. Rose told her mother that they would be headed over to Mitzi's house after their yard work ... so now they were free to tackle their mystery without checking in with anyone's parents.

"What in tarnation is the Mitzi crew doing here?" Mr. Moore cocked his head to the side and looked at Mitzi for an answer.

"You see, Mr. Moore, we have a problem and you are the only one that we trust to help us," said Mitzi.

"I sure can have a listen and try." He took a long swig from his glass.

Mitzi took a deep breath. "I think that my dad is part of a secret club that fights supernatural…"

Mr. Moore sprayed out a mouthful of tea in shock and surprise. "Shh. Get inside the house … quick … quick!"

Mr. Moore corralled the three into the house and looked down both sides of the country road with a look of alarm, before closing the door. He motioned for the kids to sit in the living room and closed the blinds and drew the curtains shut. Mitzi and Rose shared a look of worried curiosity at Mr. Moore's behavior. Finn's eyes were wide and his face a bit paler than usual.

Mr. Moore finally sat down in an old beat-up chair across from them and in a shaky, hushed voice, asked, "Can you tell me what you know?"

"I think my dad may be part of a group called The Society for Hiding Undesirable Truths, or, at least, my great grandfather was, and now my parents are in trouble." Mitzi's voice sounded worried, and she was fighting back tears.

Mr. Moore sat for a moment, carefully considering his next question. "What makes you think that this society exists? How did you hear about it?" he asked seriously.

"I guess I will start at the beginning." Mitzi sighed.

Over the next several minutes, Mitzi told the story of the shiny box with the stamp, the portrait, the map clues, the strange overheard conversations, and the book. She spoke quickly and without interruption, overwhelmed by a sense of urgency to get to the point so they could do something to help her parents.

"...and my dad just left that note!" she finished.

Finn shifted on his spot on the couch. "Please tell her this isn't real, Mr. Moore." Mitzi glanced over at Finn as he rolled his eyes.

"Well, I could tell her that," Mr. Moore looked at Finn, "but I would be lying."

"Oh man," Rose let out softly.

"What do we do now?" Mitzi asked.

"The problem is that I don't know what enemy we are dealing with here, kids. I'm too old to fight anymore, and you aren't members. By the time anyone from SHUT gets here to help, it could be too late and…"

"SHUT? What is SHUT, and what do you mean you are too old to fight *anymore*?" Rose interrupted.

"You know, The Society for Hiding Undesirable Truths. S...H...U...T ... SHUT. I was a member of SHUT and I was commander of the guards. It was my duty to protect the entrance to the Den." He looked proud.

"Where is the Den, Mr. Moore? What happens if something has taken over my mom and she gets in there somehow?" Mitzi was trying to sound calm but was completely terrified at the thought of her mother not being her mother anymore.

"The Den is underground," Mr. Moore said. "The door is in your father's office ... and I don't mean to frighten you kids, but if your mom creature gets inside the Den, the safety of your mom

130

and dad are the least of our problems." He rubbed his hands over his eyes.

"What do you mean, Mr. Moore?" Rose moved to the edge of her seat.

"I mean," he took turns looking each kid in the eyes as he spoke, "if she gets in the Den, the whole world is in serious trouble. We need a plan."

Chapter Fifteen

The four sat around Mr. Moore's Kitchen table eating cucumber sandwiches and devising their plan to save the world. They were a strange group of accidental heroes: A toothless old man, and three middle-schoolers.

At 2:45, Mr. Moore slowly pushed his chair out from the table and stood. "Okay, you guys ... looks like it's go time."

***

Mr. Moore pulled his old station wagon into his normal spot in front of Mitzi's house and took a deep breath before heading inside. "Keep it together, old man," he grumbled under his breath. He had dropped the kids off on the side of the road, just out of sight. The plan was for him to keep Mitzi's mother, well ... the thing that was supposed to be Mitzi's mother ... occupied and distracted long enough for the kids to get into the Den.

Mr. Moore slowly pushed the front door open, and was surprised to see the house looked like it had been ransacked. To the right, the living room cushions were torn open and fluff was scattered everywhere. Books had been pulled from the shelves and strewn about the room. Ahead of him in the hall, the drawers had been pulled out of the dresser and dumped onto the floor.

"DEB!" Mr Moore yelled out. "You okay?" He stood still to listen for a reply.

"Oh. Um ... Yes..." a female voice came from the office. "I'm in the office," she said. "I'll be right out!" Mr. Moore started toward the office and was taken back when he spotted Deb. Her hair and clothes were a crumpled mess, and she had a crazed look in her eyes.

"I am sorry, sir. Was I expecting you?" the she-creature said.

Sir? Mr. Moore was frozen. She had never called him sir. *I think those kids may be right. This isn't Deb. I'll need to be careful here, though. I can't let her know that I'm on to her!* Fact of the matter was Mr. Moore has been stopping by at three o'clock every day for almost three years now, but he was going to try to make it sound like something they had just arranged.

"But Deb," he smiled, "you invited me just yesterday for three o'clock tea today, remember? If it's a bad time…"

"Oh, that's right!" She tried to appear calm. "Come in … come in. We will have our tea!"

"Sounds good. Did you lose something?" Mr. Moore asked as they went to the kitchen.

"Why do you ask that?" Deb replied while making the tea with her back to him.

"It's just that the house is looking pretty … umm … torn up, you know! Looks like you've been robbed." He tried to sound casual.

"Oh that." She let out a small, nervous laugh. "I seem to have misplaced my house key. I must have lost my mind a little when I was looking for it."

"I should say so." Mr. Moore didn't want to push but couldn't help himself. "Did you find it?"

"Um yes…" she said. "It was in my purse the whole time, stupid me." She turned and flashed a toothy fake smile at Mr. Moore.

A soft creaking noise alerted Mr. Moore that the kids were trying to sneak into the house. With all of the creativity he could muster, the old man started to cough and hack and grumble as hard and as loud as he could to cover the sounds of their entrance.

Looking a bit panicked, Deb scrambled to get the coughing guest some water. "My word! Are you okay, sir? Have some water!"

He listened as best as he could and stopped his ridiculous coughing fit as soon as he was sure the kids were closed inside the office. "Yep...yep...yep," he said. "I'm just fine. I get them coughing fits from time to time you know ... getting old ... dang allergies."

She placed a steaming cup of tea in front of Mr. Moore and sat across the table with her own cup. She looked completely exhausted. *Now I just need to find a way to trick her into getting out of the house*, Mr. Moore thought to himself.

A great idea struck him, and he sat up straighter in his chair. "You know, Deb, If I was younger, or even just a bit stronger, I would love to go out and see the new entrance." He tried to seem natural as he spoke.

"New Entrance?" Deb asked.

"You know... The new entrance to..." He moved his head closer to hers and whispered, "The Den."

"OH!" Deb's eyes widened. "Right. Yes ... quite a hike. Why do you think that spot was chosen?" She was fishing for information.

"I think hiding the Den at the stream was a great idea. That little cave is so hard to find. You would never think there is a whole secret room there inside of it. But we really shouldn't be talking about all this out in the open." Mr. Moore was sure that was just enough fake information to keep her away for at least a couple of hours.

"Yes ... quite right." She nodded.

Mr. Moore tipped back the rest of his still very hot tea and pushed his chair back and stood up. "I am so sorry to cut short our tea today, Deb, but I just remembered I forgot to take my afternoon pills."

"Oh, that's okay, sir." Deb looked relieved. "Another time then." Deb stood to walk him out.

He motioned for her to sit back down. "No...no...no...sit down. Enjoy your tea! I can show myself out." As he passed the office door, he stopped to listen for a short moment. Nothing. *They must have made it into the Den.*

He drove down the driveway and turned toward the direction of his home. As soon as his car was out of sight from the house, he pulled over to the side of the road and got out with a pair of old binoculars. He hobbled over to a spot in the trees that he could see the house from and took a good look through the old lenses.

As planned, there was Deb, marching through the field, toward the stream at the edge of the property...Mr. Moore wondered how long she would stay out there searching for the entrance to a cave that didn't really exist. He felt hopeful as he got back into the car to wait for the kids.

Hopefully, they were having as much luck with their plan as he had with his.

CHAPTER SIXTEEN

Mitzi, Rose, and Finn watched as Mr. Moore drove toward the house. "I sure hope he can keep her distracted long enough for us to get in the Den." Mitzi looked concerned.

Finn pushed his glasses up his nose.

"I don't know about this…" he said. "This whole situation makes me so nervous." He twitched as he spoke.

Rose put her hand on her hip and turned to face Finn. "We got this, Finny. We get in, find out what we can from the Den, and get the hell out of there. It's simple."

Mitzi started walking toward her house and motioned for her two friends to follow. "Alright, you two, no more talking until we are safe in the Den."

They tip toed up the front steps, trying not to make a sound. Mitzi put her face against the door, trying hard to hear if anyone was still around. She couldn't hear anything, so she was pretty sure Mr. Moore had gotten Deb into the kitchen to make tea as planned.

As she turned the doorknob and slowly pushed the door open, the silence was broken by the sound of a small *ca-reek*. Mitzi froze in fear but was able to quickly relax as sounds of Mr. Moore's genius coughing fit flooded through the hall.

"Run!" Mitzi mouthed to Rose and Finn and the three moved as quickly and quietly to the office as they possibly could. Rose turned to shut the door behind her just as the coughing fit disappeared back into silence.

Mitzi stood behind her father's large desk. "Mr. Moore said the entrance is under the desk, but

I don't see anything here!" Mitzi ran her fingers through her hair in exasperation.

"See if the floorboards are loose!" Finny suggested in a somewhat louder-than-he-should-have whisper.

"Shush." Rose shot Finn an angry look. "Keep your dang voice down or you'll get us caught."

Mitzi was on her hands and knees, running her fingers along the edges of the wood planks of the floor, gently trying to lift each one free but with no success.

"Try under the chair!" Finn offered in more reasonable hushed tones.

"Good idea."

Mitzi turned around, and the second board she tested sprang free from the floor. The other planks around it held firm so Mitzi was confused. *What am I missing here? A cat couldn't even fit into that hole. Maybe there is something inside*? She looked up at Finn and Rose and shrugged her shoulders before reaching her hand into the dark hole where the board used to be. It was deeper than she expected. Her arm sank into the floor just past her elbow when her fingers hit what felt like a hard metal object. Mitzi could feel excitement buzz through her body as she lifted the mysterious thing from its hiding place. It was a metal box about the size of a cell phone. It was smooth and silver and the three looked at it and had no idea what it was or even what to do with it. Mitzi turned it around again and again in her hand, searching for a button or a way to turn it on. No luck.

"Try tapping on it maybe?" Rose suggested.

Mitzi shrugged and gave the object a couple of hard taps. The edge of the object lit up a soft red glow in Mitzi's hand, surprising her, and she almost dropped it.

"Look!" she whispered as the word Passcode appeared on its surface in a blue light.

"Mr. Moore didn't say anything about a passcode!" Rose was panicking.

Mitzi took a deep breath. "Finn, was there anything in the guidebook about a code?"

"Not that I can recall." Finn said. "Was there anything on that stamp you found?"

"Just FC." Mitzi said. "That's hardly a code, right?"

"Well," Finn said, pushing his glasses up his nose, "It says passCODE and not passWORD, so I have a feeling we need a…"

"A NUMBER!" Mitzi interrupted in hushed excitement. "I bet it's 335! Remember? The time in the painting! But there are no buttons on this thing! Where do I put it?"

"Maybe you need to tap it?" Rose bit her lip.

"Okay, I'll try."

tap...tap...tap…

tap...tap...tap…

tap...tap...tap...tap...tap…

NOTHING.

"Hey, let me try something." Rose took the object from Mitzi and, using her finger like a pen, wrote the number 335 across its surface. The red light rim turned green and one loud click came from the area under the desk.

The three stood back, eyes wide as the desk and the section of the floor underneath it, lifted about a foot off the floor and then without making even the slightest sound, glided back about three feet, revealing a dark entrance.

"How in the world did I not know this was here?" Mitzi looked down at the dark spiral stone staircase.

"I don't know, but we need to get moving!" Rose sounded alarmed. "I think I just heard Mr. Moore say that he was leaving!"

One at a time, the three stepped down into the unknown. With every step, the path grew colder and darker. As Mitzi stepped from the last step onto the solid floor, the little bit of light remaining faded to black. Mitzi stood scrambling to find her flashlight in her bag as lights started clicking on in rapid succession.

"That's convenient!" Finn smiled and nodded at the tunnel ahead. In front of them was a long stone tunnel with a stone floor. The ceiling was arched and spotted with ornate hanging lamps about every ten feet or so.

"I hope this path doesn't have any booby traps," Rose said nervously.

"Good point," Mitzi said. "We better be cautious and look carefully as we go."

Ahead, the stone tunnel curved to the right and as they turned the corner, a large metal circular door came into view. It looked like one of those old bank vault doors you might see in an old cowboy movie.

"Holy crap!" Finn pushed his glasses up his nose as the three moved closer to the door.

"I can't believe this is even happening." Rose was shaking her head. "I mean, this is crazy. Look at this thing."

On the door, there were dozens of small, indented circles, each with a different animal picture etched into them. There was no handle and no other buttons…

"Well, this is odd," Mitzi said

"Yep. What the hell do we do now?" Rose asked.

"I don't know. But let's look at these closely and try to figure this out," Mitzi said. Finn started naming aloud the animals in each of the circles. "Frog, cat, deer, elephant, bird, kangaroo. This Doesn't make any sense at all!" He sounded frustrated but kept going. "Rat, sheep, fox, cow, whale, pig, horse…"

"WAIT!" Rose put her hand up in excitement. "I think I have an idea! Mitzi, your great grandfather was always reading a book that he loved enough to put clues in, right? I'm thinking that maybe the whale is significant then, right? Wasn't that book about some kind of whale?"

Mitzi smiled a big smile. "Yes, of course. 'MOBY DICK'! Great thinking, Rose."

148

"Actually," Finn cleared his throat, "most people think that 'Moby Dick' was about the whale, but in actuality it's a story about a man's relationship with…"

"NOW IS NOT THE TIME, FINNY!" Rose snapped.

"Okay...okay…" Finn relented. "So, what do we do? Press the whale and see what happens?"

Mitzi reached her hand forward with her pointer finger, leading the way to the circle with the whale. As she pressed it, the circle glowed a red glow and a soft buzzing noise came from the door.

"Well, that didn't work. Now what?" Mitzi was getting discouraged.

"I wish this was just a normal door…" Rose whined. "With a normal lock … and a normal key…"

"What are we missing here?" Mitzi thought out loud as she pressed her face up close to the circle with the whale in it.

She ran her finger over the whale and the circle once again glowed a red glow. She ran her finger around the rim of the circle and noticed two tiny wedges poking out from the top right side of the circle. Her face flushed as she realized that the whale circle was the lock and that she had the key! Only, she didn't know she had the key until now. She had thought it was some kind of stamp all along. She pulled the silver FC stamp, well ... key out of her bag and held it up to show her friends.

"Don't worry, guys... I think we have a key!" Mitzi held her breath as she lined the flat end of the key up to the whale lock and turned it slightly to match the notches in the key to the wedges in the lock.

SNAP! The key stuck firmly in place and the whole door glowed a soft green glow as it buzzed and rolled up into a giant slot in the stone ceiling that they hadn't noticed before.

"Mitzi, you, my friend, are a genius," Finn proclaimed.

But neither Mitzi nor Rose could speak. The shock of discovering the Den that lay before them had rendered them speechless.

CHAPTER SEVENTEEN

The room was massive ... like the size of a high school gymnasium. But instead of bleachers and basketball hoops, the three were surrounded by shelves filled with mountains of books and strange looking artifacts, and row after row of tiny wooden drawers filled with who-knows-what. In the center of the den was a long table with at least thirty chairs around it. At the far end, papers lay scattered on its surface. The far wall was a giant grid of photos and maps and notes, the kind of display you might see on one of those crime solving TV shows.

Mitzi noticed four separate doors in the back of the room and wondered where they each led.

On the right shelves, she noticed carved boxes, glass vials filled with mysterious glowing liquids, golden pyramid shaped statues, and other crazy looking trinkets living amongst volumes and volumes of old leather-bound books. To her left, she strained to read the labels on the little drawers ... powdered moonstone … hummingbird blood … widow's tears... Her mind raced. *What are all of these crazy looking things?*

"Come on, guys!" Mitzi said with a stern voice. "Let's see what all those papers are down at the end of the table. I have a feeling that most of the information that we need will be there."

As they approached the end of the table, Mitzi noticed a map of Hanford with a red circle on it about halfway down county road 6. *I knew it. The Halberts have something to do with this mess. But what?*

"Umm Mitz?" Finn's eyes grew wide as he read silently from a paper in his hands. "I know what kind of creatures we are dealing with. They are Mimics."

Rose and Mitzi looked at each other and, in ironic unison, asked, "What is a Mimic?"

"This paper just says…

NUBRAS Registration Change Form

Halbert, OPEN file #6742,

New Residence: County Road 6, Hanford, NY.

Family of 3

Class A Non-human: Mimic

"I think that we should check the guidebook!" He put the paper back on the table.

The three pulled chairs close together around the end of the table and Mitzi got the guidebook out of her bag and set it on the table between them. She flipped through the creatures section until she found the pages for Mimics.

She cleared her throat before reading the descriptions out loud.

"Mimics are generally recognized as safe. They have the ability to morph into another being, human and animal. Change requires only a single drop of blood from the creature being copied. Mimics can keep in form as long as the original creature is living. The true form of a mimic is a shifting and grey jelly-like blob with several protruding sharp spikes."

"That's creepy," Rose said.

"There is good news there, though," Finn added. "They didn't kill your parents! Otherwise, they wouldn't be able to stay morphed as them."

"I agree." Mitzi was slightly relieved. She looked back down into the guidebook and started to read again.

"To force a mimic to release from the morphed creature's identity, there are only three options. One: convince them to change on their own. Two: kill them, which can be tricky to distinguish between the original and the copy. Three: use knotgrass."

"I think it's safe to say that we really only have two options." Rose looked worried. "I sure as hell aint killin' no one...creature or otherwise."

"Same," added Finn.

"I guess we better figure out this knotgrass thing then because I'm not too confident that we can convince them to give me my parents back." Mitzi flipped through the guidebook until she found the listing for knotgrass.

"This common plant of the dock family, knotgrass, has jointed creeping stems and small pink flowers. Its greens can be dried and powdered, and its flowers can be steeped into tonic or distilled as an essence. Will force a Mimic back to its true form. Mild sedative to Rargolls. Always in Inventory."

Mitzi nodded to the wall of tiny drawers. "Guess we better find us some knotgrass."

They were swift in finding the knotgrass, all thankful that the drawers were organized in alphabetical order. When they pulled out the long, skinny drawer they saw one neat row of little brown bottles with liquid inside and one row of little leather drawstring bags. It looked like a few of the bags had been removed and the three agreed that Mitzi's dad must have taken some out.

"I say we each take a bottle and a bag...and maybe one of each for Mr. Moore, too," Finn suggested.

"Good thinking, Finn," said Mitzi. "I don't think there is such a thing as being over prepared for something like this. Let's pack up my bag and get out of here. I hope Mr. Moore has got things covered for us up there."

As the three made their way back out of the Den, Mitzi took one last look into the giant room and hoped that one day she would have the chance to discover all of its secrets…

CHAPTER EIGHTEEN

As they stepped into the stone passageway, the door to the Den automatically rolled down from the slot in the ceiling and snapped back into place. The three jogged down the path in silence, with an unspoken sense of urgency. When they arrived at the spiral staircase, Mitzi placed her foot on the bottom step and the lights went out. A crack of light trickled through from above as the desk parted from the floor.

"Wow!" exclaimed Finn. "This whole place has got some seriously cool technology going on."

"We gotta be quiet now, guys," Mitzi warned as she popped her head into the open of her father's office. She sat on the floor and retrieved the silver key box from her bag and tucked it back into the floorboards where she had found it, carefully putting the plank back in place. The desk silently shifted back over the opening to the staircase as the three headed to the door.

Before Rose could turn the handle, the door flew open and before them stood a wide-eyed and angry creature, in the shape of Mitzi's mother Deb. Monster Deb was breathing heavily through clenched teeth. Her hands and face were muddy and so were her pants. Her hair was a disheveled mess. The three froze at the sight of her, a bit terrified and unsure how to proceed.

"WHAT ARE YOU BRATS DOING IN HERE?" She snarled.

Mitzi tried to come up with a story as fast as she could. She could feel her heart pounding in her ears.

"We were looking for you," she blurted out. Monster Deb looked at her suspiciously but didn't say anything, so Mitzi continued. "I wanted to spend the night at Rose's house but didn't pack a bag and couldn't find you so…"

"YOU ARE LYING!" monster Deb yelled. "I can smell it."

"We aren't lying … we aren't lying." Finn nervously shook his head as he subconsciously backed away from Monster Deb.

"You three are working with the old man." She stepped toward them, pushing them back into the corner of the room as she spoke. "That stupid old fool had me digging for nothing so you brats could get in here and spoil my plans."

"We don't know what you're talking about!" Rose pleaded.

"No. We don't know what you're talking about…" Monster Deb mimicked Rose in a crazed and high pitched voice.

"What plan?" Mitzi asked as bravely as she could despite the lump of fear in her throat.

Monster Deb snapped her neck to face Mitzi and brought her nose down to the tip of Mitzi's nose. Her breath felt hot and smelled like a rotten sewer drain.

"Oh, you damn Clarks think you are so special." She grabbed Mitzi's chin and pulled her even closer. "You think that you can keep all these juicy little secrets to yourself. Well, you are *wrong*. The OPEN will win. We will!" She pushed Mitzi so hard that she crashed into Rose, who stumbled back into Finn. The three of them fell hard to the floor. With that, Monster Deb let out a low and sinister laugh.

The laugh sent chills through Mitzi's whole body. She was scared and disgusted all rolled into one. She knew that the monster before her was not really her mother, but she looked and sounded exactly like her. The whole thing was so hard to process. *If I could just get in my bag without her noticing maybe I can get to the knotgrass. But then what? What do I do? Think, Mitz...think...think...*

Monster Deb took a few steps back to the corner of the desk and picked up a heavy looking iron table lamp that had a round marble base. As she yanked the chord to unplug it, the mosaic glass shade snapped off and crashed to the floor, sending colorful shards of glass in every direction. Her face contorted into a dramatic sad expression.

"Oh no. Boo hoo. Was that old?" she teased. "I didn't need that part, anyway." Her fake cry baby face changed to an evil and serious looking sneer. "It

163

will work just fine like this. Yes. This will beat you all to death with no problem."

"What? NO! Why?" cried Rose

"We didn't do anything!" cried Finn.

"They have nothing to do with this," pleaded Mitzi. "Please, just let them go. Your fight is with me...not them."

Monster Deb stood grasping the lamp as she pretended to consider Mitzi's request. "I can't let them go now." She shrugged her shoulders. "They know too much. But I will promise to make their deaths quick. Just as long as you tell me what I need to know...and I need to know how to get into the Den."

"We will never tell you anything." Mitzi started to stand.

"That's right," Finn agreed.

"Yes. Screw you," Rose said as she and Finn stood beside their friend.

"Well, I guess I will just have to kill you all then." She lifted the lamp high above her just as a shovel smashed down on her head from behind, knocking her into an unconscious pile on the floor.

"Mr. Moore," Rose was shaken and breathing fast, "I have never been so excited to see you in my life!"

"That was excellent timing for sure," added Finn as Mitzi gave Mr. Moore a warm and thankful smile.

"Oh crap. Do I need to sit down," Mr. Moore said as he hobbled over to the desk chair and sat. "I saw that Deb monster thingy make her way back toward the house and knew you three buffoons were still inside. What in god's name took you so long?" He took a deep breath and scratched his face.

Finn kicked Monster Deb's leg to be sure she was good and out of it. "We had to figure out how to get in...and then where to go....and then how to open the door...and then…"

"Never mind!" Mr. Moore snapped. "Mitzi, get some strong tape so we can secure this creature here. We can't have her waking up and getting in our way."

"But if it wakes up... Can't it just morph into its true form to get free from the tape?" asked Rose.

"True form … Hmmm… So, I'm thinking you guys figured out that we are dealing with Mimics then. Well, I suppose it could morph. But, without a human or animal around, it really wouldn't want to. They can't move too well in their true form. Besides that, I hit her pretty darn hard. I expect she will be out for several hours. And then Mitz … after we save your parents, they will know what to do with her."

"You mean *if* we save my parents, right?" Mitzi felt overwhelmed by the task in front of them. She was so scared that they wouldn't be able to save them.

"No, Mitzo. I meant *when* we save your parents." Mr. Moore gave her a hopeful and kind smile. "Now...go get that tape so we can secure this piece of crap and get out of here!"

Chapter Nineteen

With Monster Deb taped firmly to a kitchen chair, the four piled into Mr. Moore's old station wagon in silence. Mr. Moore started up the old car and sat thinking for a moment.

"So, you guys got some knotgrass, and you know the address of the Halbert's house...but do any of you have a good plan in mind?" Mr. Moore asked as he stared blankly out his window and off into the distance.

Mitzi bit the inside of her cheek, deep in thought. "I was hoping you had a few ideas." .

"Well…" The old man sounded tired "If we could come up with some kind of diversion or a way to get inside…"

"Not to mention, we need a plan once we are in there," Finn added.

"I think I may have an idea!" Rose leaned forward from her seat in the back. "Mitzi, do you have any of those fundraiser chocolate bars leftover that we are supposed to sell for summer drama club camp?"

"Yeah. They're in my room. Haven't sold any yet, actually. Why?" Mitzi answered.

"I think I have a plan to create a diversion and maybe even get one of them to morph into their true form at the same time." Rose sounded confident.

"I think I see where you're going with this," said Finn.

"Yeah. We are selling the chocolate door-to-door and are offering free samples. Well, two of us...and the other two can sneak around and look for another way inside."

Mr. Moore scratched his chin. "I suppose that could work," he said. "Then what do we do if the damn thing doesn't eat a sample? What if it takes the sample and morphs in the doorway and that alerts whatever other creatures are inside and they attack us? Your idea was good thinking, Rose, but I think we need to avoid morphing one of them into a true form until we really know what we are up against. Like how many are really inside."

"According to that registration paper we found in the Den, there are only three mimics living there … and one is currently duct taped to the kitchen chair, so that should mean there are only two left, don't you think?" Rose questioned the group.

"But what if there are more?" Mitzi asked. "We should have a plan for a group of them just in case." The car fell silent again just as little drops of rain started to fall from the sky that made soft plinking sounds as they bounced off the roof.

"Seems to me that we need a reconnaissance mission." Finn shrugged.

"What do you mean, Finny?" Mr. Moore looked intrigued.

"Well, seems like before we can come up with a rescue plan, we need to know what we're up against. You know ... surveillance," he said.

The three nodded in agreement.

"So...?" Rose was impatient.

"So ... we use the whole chocolate selling door to door bit as a way to get inside!" He smiled.

Rose let out a sigh and leaned back into her seat. "They ain't just gonna let us in because we're selling chocolates. They'll probably just slam the door in our faces."

"Just wait a moment, Rose," said Mr. Moore. "I think our man Finn is onto something here." He started strumming the steering wheel with his fingertips as the sky opened up, dumping buckets of rain.

"Mitzi, go inside and get those chocolate bars. I will fill you guys in on the way!" He was practically yelling with excitement. "And grab an umbrella while you're in there."

Chapter Twenty

Nervously, Rose closed her umbrella and knocked three times on the Halbert's front door. She stood hugging her fundraiser box of chocolate bars and could feel her heart racing wildly through the cardboard. The door creaked open and a tall, balding, skinny man stood smiling at her.

"What can I do for you, young lady?" he asked.

"Good afternoon, sir." She cleared her throat. "My name is Rose Brown, and I am selling chocolate bars to raise money for my summer camp tuition. Would you like to buy some, please? They are three bucks each or two for five."

The man's smile faded as he looked over Rose's head at Mr. Moore's car in the driveway. Mitzi and Finn were hiding in the back seat and Mr. Moore was wearing a baseball cap, low over his eyes. It was still raining quite heavily, and it was nearly impossible to see into the car at all. Rose turned and waved at Mr. Moore with a big cheesy grin on her face.

"Oh, that's just my dad," she said.

"I suppose I can buy a couple of bars. Let me go and get some cash," he said as he shut the door and disappeared into the house. Rose tried to peek into the windows, but they had heavy curtains up, blocking every bit of space from view. The door opened and the man thrust a five dollar bill out in front of Rose. "I'll just take two."

Rose took the money from him and pulled two bars out of the box and handed them to the man. "Thank you so much, sir!" she said. He turned to go and started to shut the door behind him just as Rose blurted out "I'm sorry. Excuse me, sir?"

The man turned to face Rose again, this time looking annoyed and impatient. "Now what?" he grumbled.

"I really don't mean to be a bother but I am having a bit of an emergency and I really…" She lowered her voice to a whisper, "…need to use the bathroom." She tried to make her face look as pathetic and desperate as possible.

"I don't think I like the idea of some kid that I don't even know going into my home and…" He rolled his eyes.

"Please, sir. I don't think I can hold it all the way back into town. I won't touch a thing, I promise. I wouldn't ask if it wasn't an emergency. You seem like such a nice person and I thought you would understand. I don't know if I can hold it much longer at all and…."

"OH, FOR CRYIN' OUT LOUD … hang on," he complained as he closed the door and disappeared into the house again.

Rose turned and flashed Mr. Moore a thumbs up. A few short moments later, the man returned and showed her to the bathroom. Rose tried to take in every detail as she made the short walk to the bathroom. To her right, she passed an empty sitting room that looked just like a regular run-of-the-mill room, unremarkable in every way. On her left was a staircase, followed by what looked to be a closet door on the side of it.

"Here you go," he said. "Make it snappy." He pointed to the door on the right.

Rose noticed a closed door on the left, opposite the bathroom. She thought to herself, *I bet that's the kitchen.* "Oh, I will be super fast! Thanks again, Mr…?" Rose smiled at the man.

"Halbert. Now get a move on it!" he barked.

In the bathroom, Rose tried to listen for any bits of sound coming from anywhere in the house but didn't hear any at all. There was a small window, facing the back yard and as she flushed the unused toilet, she clicked the lever to the unlocked position and washed her hands. Mr. Halbert was standing right outside the door waiting for her and as she stepped into the hallway, she started dramatically clearing her throat and then started coughing as severely and realistically as she could.

"Water! Please!" she choked out between coughs.

"Oh brother! Don't move." Mr. Halbert pushed past her and into the kitchen, careful to shut the door behind him. Lucky for Rose, she got just enough of a glimpse inside the kitchen to see someone familiar sitting at the table.

Mr. Halbert returned with a small glass of water and Rose took a teeny sip from it. "Much better!" Rose smiled and handed the glass back to Mr. Halbert. "Thanks again, for everything!" she yelled as she stepped outside and opened her umbrella.

He stood watching as she ran through the rain. "Thank you ... for reminding me to be glad that I never had children. Pain in the rear...the whole lot of you!" he mumbled under his breath as he watched her get into the car to leave.

"I am so glad that is over!" Rose proclaimed as she sat down in the front seat and closed the door.

"What did you find out?" Mitzi asked from her spot huddled on the backseat floor.

"Not really a whole lot." Rose shrugged. "The house seemed pretty empty, and that dude was kind of a grouch. I did manage to unlock the bathroom window, at least. It faces the back yard and didn't seem too high of the ground. When I came out of the bathroom, I faked a coughing fit and when Mr. Halbert went to get me some water, I caught a glimpse of that chubby lawyer guy that was missing before…"

"Do you mean Martin?" Mitzi asked.

"Yes! That's his name. Couldn't remember it…yeah."

"You guys can sit up now. We're clear of the house," Mr. Moore said. He added, "We can pull into the old church parking lot up ahead and figure out what to do next."

Finn sat up and stretched. "So, the only people you saw were Mr. Halbert and Martin? Hmmm…I'm sure both of them are Mimics. Hopefully, they are the only ones there. Do you think they just have the real Halberts and our people tied up somewhere in the house?" he asked.

"I guess that we will just have to assume that is the truth," Mr. Moore said as he pulled into the church lot and parked the car. "We just need a way to get them out of the house so that we can get in there and get our people out!"

"I have an idea," said Mitzi. "Mr. Moore can call Martin pretending to be from SHUT and say there is an emergency meeting in the Den. That will get at least one of them out of there, and it will give us at least 30 minutes to get in and out."

"But what do we do if one of them stays behind?" Rose asked.

"Well...I don't expect it would stand a chance against all four of us...and we have knotgrass, too," Mr. Moore said.

"Two of us can sneak in through the bathroom window and let the other two in the front door," Finn said. "Then we can look for our people and hopefully get out of there quickly!"

"Well, it certainly isn't the best plan I have ever heard, but it's all we got, so I say, let's get a move on." Mr. Moore turned to look at the three kids. "Now, which one of you has a phone? I have a call I need to make."

"One small problem…" Rose mumbled. "I have a phone, but I definitely don't have Martin's phone number."

"Oh crap," Mitzi said. "I didn't think of that."

"I got that covered," Mr. Moore said as he reached into his inside jacket pocket and pulled out a small black notepad and unclipped a mini pen from its cover and started flipping through the pages. "I keep track of all of the members...just in case a situation like this arises and I need to get hold of someone and such... Oh, yes...here it is."

Rose carefully dialed the number and handed Mr. Moore the phone.

Mr. Moore sat up straight in his seat and looked a bit nervous. "Is this Martin? This is Moore. Central headquarters is requesting an emergency meeting for a code 6120. One hour. In the Den. I was unable to reach Ben Clark, and I have several other calls to make. Can you reach out to him? Great. I will see you and Mr. Clark at the Den in one hour's time."

"That was awesome, Mr. Moore!" Finn said, clearly impressed. "What the heck is a code 6120?"

Mr. Moore chuckled to himself. "I have no idea. I just made it up."

"Oh, I get it," said Finn. "You just called a Mimic, not the real Martin...so he won't know that you've made it up, right?"

"Exactly. Now let's see where we can hide this beast of a car while we wait for them to leave."

Chapter Twenty-One

They were lucky enough to find a large bulldozer collecting dust on the shoulder of the country road...just a bit farther down from the Halbert's driveway. Mr. Moore pulled the car behind the big machine to shield them from view. If Mitzi leaned back into her seat as far as possible, she could just make out the end of the driveway through an opening in the treads of the old dozer.

"Anything yet?" Rose was anxious.

"Not yet," said Mitzi

"Are you three sure that you can handle this?" Mr. Moore asked, looking tired and nervous.

"I'm not gonna lie," Finn said, "I kinda feel like I could barf right now."

"Same," Rose added. "But we can handle this."

"What choice do we really have?" asked Mitzi. "I mean, we *have* to keep this all a secret, so we can't call the police...and we don't even really know if other local society members have been replaced with Mimics!"

"Yeah…" Finn scratched his head. "About that... Umm, Mr. Moore...ummm...how do we really know you aren't a Mimic, too...leading us into a trap?" He shrugged his shoulders and his face flushed red with embarrassment.

"Oh, for crying out loud, Finn!" Rose scolded.

"No...no…" Mr. Moore nodded his head. "Our young man has a point. Someone give me their vial of knotgrass essence, so I can put his doubts to bed."

Finn handed his vial to Mr. Moore, who opened it, shook a few drops into the palm of his hand, and licked it. "There!" Mr. Moore scowled. "I'm still me. Now, don't make me do that again! That tasted like rat piss!"

The nervousness they were all feeling backed down a bit as the three laughed at Mr. Moore's description.

"How do you know what rat piss tastes like?" teased Rose.

"Oh, shut up." Mr. Moore chuckled.

"Hey, you guys. I hate to break up the party but it looks like someone is leaving!" Mitzi squinted her eyes and moved her face in closer to the glass. "I think I see two people in the car!"

"Finally some good news." Mr. Moore sounded a bit relieved. "We will wait five more minutes, just to be sure...then you're up, Finn and Mitz."

***

"House looks pretty still from here," Mitzi whispered to Finn as they double timed it down the driveway toward the house. They had decided to leave the car in its safe spot behind the bulldozer so that Mr. Moore could watch in case the Mimics came back early. Rose would follow ten minutes behind Finn and Mitzi and go in the front door.

"I just want to get to the back window!" Finn complained. "I feel so damn exposed out here. If there *is* anything still inside...they already see us and that is freakin' me out."

Mitzi nodded. "Yeah. Me too. Let's just hope we are right and all of these monsters are at my house."

"That's funny, Mitz." Finn laughed.

187

"What's funny?" Mitzi asked.

"You just said that you hope all the monsters are at your house." Finn snorted as he pushed his glasses back up his sweaty nose.

"Hilarious…" Mitzi said, clearly unamused.

As they came upon the house, they took a moment to peek into the front window. It seemed to both of them that the place was empty. The sitting room looked dark and there was no movement inside at all. They went around to the back of the house to the place Rose had said the bathroom window was. The bottom of the window was just out of Mitzi's reach but, luckily, they found some old milk crates in the yard that were just sturdy and tall enough to work. It took a few minutes to get inside. Mitzi went first and accidentally kicked Finn square in the nose.

"Damn it, Mitz." He squealed in pain and grabbed his face as blood started dripping from his nostrils.

"I'm sorry, Finn!" Mitzi said as she passed a wad of toilet paper out of the bathroom window to him.

"Maybe the swelling will keep my glasses from sliding down my nose..." Finn said as the glasses slid down his nose again. "...or maybe not." Finn stuffed bits of tissue in his nostrils and pulled himself, quite ungracefully, into the bathroom. "Okay. We are in. Now what?" Finn asked as he closed the window behind him.

"Now, we open the front door for Rose and find my parents as quickly as possible," Mitzi whispered back as she cracked open the bathroom door and took a careful look into the house.

She pressed her finger to her lips and then motioned for Finn to follow as she tiptoed out into the main hall of the house. The floor creaked and moaned underneath their every step, so they stopped several times along the way and stood still to listen for any sounds. Finn opened the front door and was relieved to see Rose standing there waiting.

"Hey guys! I take it we are good to go?" Rose whispered.

"We think so," Mitzi whispered back. "But let's search in silence just in case."

"Yes. I want to get out of here quickly! Let's split up," Rose suggested.

"Good idea," Mitzi agreed. "I'll look down here, and you two check upstairs. If you find anyone, knock twice on a wall or floor until we know for sure this place is safe."

"What do we do if we come across a Mimic?" Finn's eyes were wide, and he was nervously shifting his weight back and forth.

"You just yell like hell, and we will come running to help," Rose answered.

"Right. Plus, remember, Mr. Moore is watching the driveway and plans to rescue us if we aren't out of here in exactly…" Mitzi paused to look at her watch. "…fourteen minutes."

"Let's go then," said Rose as the three took off into the house to search for their missing people.

Chapter Twenty-Two

Mitzi glanced through the living room and opened the closet door, and found nothing even the slightest bit interesting. As she pushed open the kitchen door, a bolt of lightning surged through her body at the sight of her father, zip-tied to a kitchen chair. He had grey tape over his mouth and bruises on his face. His eyes grew wide at the shock of seeing his only child come to his rescue.

"Dad!" Mitzi yelled, forgetting to be quiet. Her father tried to reply, but the tape over his mouth made it impossible. "I'm so sorry, Dad...but this is gonna hurt, I think." Mitzi grabbed a corner of the tape and pulled it as hard and fast as she could. She could feel it pulling and ripping away at his facial hair and knew it was extremely painful. She cringed as he let out a soft moan, but he bravely tried to hide his discomfort.

"Good girl," he said. "Now...go and get one of those kitchen knives and cut my hands and feet free."

Mitzi followed his instructions as questions came flooding out of her father's mouth. "How in the heck did you find us? How did you get here? Are you alone? How did you get them out of the house? How long until they come back? Did you free your mother and the others, yet? Oh Mitzi! You've really saved the day!"

"I'll explain everything later, Dad, I promise. But for now, let's go get Mom and the others," she said as she cut the last tie. "Finn and Rose are looking for them now...but we better hurry up."

"They are in the attic!" he said as he grabbed the knife Mitzi had used to free him. They left the kitchen and rushed up the stairs. "The attic is where they kept us. They came and got me about an hour ago. The creature that was a copy of Fred Halbert dropped out of morph and turned into a copy of me. He took the monster copy of Martin with him and left...leaving me tied to the chair."

As they reached the top of the stairs, Dad pointed straight ahead to an open door. "There's the attic. I think maybe Rose and Finn may have found them already…"

"Sure did!" said Rose with a grin as she appeared on the attic stairs with a small line of people descending the steps behind her. Mitzi watched as Mr. and Mrs. Halbert stepped into the hallway, followed by an older gentleman that Mitzi assumed was Mr. Halbert's father.

Then Finn appeared with a big smile on his face followed by a grumbly and complaining Martin...and, finally, Mitzi's mom. Mitzi felt a lump form in her throat as she rushed to her and wrapped her arms tightly around her.

"I don't know how you guys did it, Mitzo, but I sure am proud of all of you," Deb said as she planted a kiss on Mitzi's head.

"Save it!" Martin snapped. "We need to get the hell outta here!"

"Yes," Dad agreed. "Let's go!" They took off down the stairs with Dad in front. But, halfway down the steps, he stopped hard and fast, sending the line of people behind him crashing into each other. He turned to face the group. "I hear a car! I think they're coming back. Mitzi...do you guys have any knotgrass, by chance?"

"Yes! We each took one vial and one bag of powder!" she answered.

"Okay, listen closely!" Her father spoke quickly and quietly. "Halberts...back to the attic! We will get you when it's clear. Martin, you and Finn, go to the back bedroom and be ready to attack with your knotgrass! Deb! You and Rose go to the kitchen and be ready as well! Mitzi and I will try to stop them out here. Go!"

Mitzi fumbled inside her pockets and pulled out the vial of knotgrass and handed it to her father. She could hear three car doors shut outside. "Mitzi, get behind that couch," her dad pointed to a nearby green sofa, "and I will try to surprise them at the door. They are here! Shhh." He flattened himself against the wall beside the door. Mitzi held her breath as she crouched behind the couch. She noticed a mirror hanging on the living room wall that allowed her to see most of the entryway. Terror ran through her as the front door creaked open and her father's Mimic walked in, followed by Martin's Mimic, and a very angry Mimic Deb.

CHAPTER TWENTY-THREE

Monster Dad rolled his head around, cracking his neck and sniffing the air. "They are still here. I can smell them."

Monster Deb and Monster Martin dramatically sniffed the air and nodded in agreement. Mitzi noticed her father still had the kitchen knife that she had used to cut him free earlier. He quickly poured knotgrass essence over the blade and stuffed the vial back into his pocket. She was scared and didn't know what he would do.

In a flash, Dad jumped toward the three Mimics and swished his knife through the air, landing his blade on Monster Deb's arm. The cut looked very small and there wasn't any blood that Mitzi could see, but the Mimic mom started to scream and shake and fell to the floor. Monster Martin took off in a frightened run toward the kitchen as Mimic Dad spun to face their attacker.

Mimic Deb continued to writhe and wiggle on the floor as a green smoke started seeping out of her eyes, ears, nose, and mouth.

Mimic Dad kicked real Dad's hand, sending the knife flying down the hall and sliding across the floor, resting under a small table. "That's great. The old blade dipped in knotgrass, huh? Clever human." Mimic Dad snarled as he and real Dad started circling each other, face to face.

"That's right!" the real dad yelled back. "And if you were clever, you'd just morph on your own and get this over with!"

"Not a chance!" the Mimic yelled as he jumped onto Dad and the two crashed onto the floor, punching and fighting. "You think you humans are so darn special. You are all a bunch of ego maniacs. You think you are so much better than us, but you are not!"

"We only treat monsters like you the way you deserve to be treated!" Mitzi's dad yelled back.

"That's bull!" grunted the mimic. "You even call us 'UNDESIRABLE CREATURES' in your stupid little society."

"Well, if the shoe fits!" Dad replied.

Mitzi held her breath as the two rolled over in a violent dance, punching and kicking each other, wishing she could help in some way.

Mitzi couldn't tell which one was her father and which was the Mimic as they struggled to dominate each other, eventually rolling out of Mitzi's view.

Mitzi watched in horror as the green smoke that was coming out from Monster Deb's face changed to a dark grey. The Mimic's skin started to bubble and boil away, revealing a gooey, blobby, slimy-looking grey substance underneath. As the rest of its skin and clothes dissolved, the blob shrank and formed into a lumpy ball of grey goo. Sharp, needle-like objects protruded out of the lumpy slime monster, and it started sliding toward Mitzi.

Mitzi could hear the dads crash into something as their fight continued in the hall. She stood and looked around for something she could use to fight off the blob that was heading her way. *They need a drop of blood to change. I can't let it stab me with one of those needle things! If I can just trap it in something!*

The blob wasn't moving very quickly, which gave Mitzi a few seconds to formulate a plan. She ran around the blob and grabbed an umbrella out of a bin near the door. She opened the coat closet to look for a bin or container she could use to trap the blob. Then an idea struck her, and she shook her head at her naivety. *I can trap it in the closet!*

She turned to see one of the dads on top of the other dad, with his hands locked around his throat. *OMG! He's going to kill him! But who is killing who? Which one is my real dad?*

Mitzi turned back toward the blob, and it was getting close! She ran around it, barely missing contact with one of its shifting needles and as hard as she could, pushed it into the closet with the handle end of the umbrella. It was much heavier and harder to push than she thought it would be, but determined, she managed to smoosh it in there. She quickly slammed the closet door closed behind it, trapping it inside.

Without hesitating, she ran to the dads and kicked at the dad that was on top of the other dad, sending him sideways and onto the ground.

"Why would you do that?" he yelled. "I was about to kill it!"

The dad that was being strangled sat up and was breathing heavily and coughing in relief. "I am your real dad, not him."

Mitzi saw the knife poking out from under the hall table and bent to pick it up. Both dads were talking at once.... pleading with Mitzi.

"It's him, not me...."

"I'm your real dad..."

Mitzi yelled, "Stop!" and both dads fell silent. "Just tell me something only my real dad would know!"

"I love you so much," said the dad that had been strangling the other dad.

"'Moby Dick'," said the sitting dad still catching his breath from the near death strangulation.

'Moby Dick'! Yes, that's my father! Mitzi turned toward the Mimic.

Sensing his defeat, the Mimic dad lunged forward, grabbing the knife from Mitzi's hand, and pushed her toward the floor and into her father.

"Now I'll just have to kill you. Normally, I would keep you...never know when a young girl would come in handy. But you've pissed me off...so you're gonna die," he said as he stepped toward them, knife in hand.

"But if you kill my dad, you will be forced into your true form," Mitzi said.

"Smart little girl." The Mimic snarled. "I'm just going to kill you and make him watch."

"No, you are NOT!" yelled Mitzi's father and he pushed her behind him with his arm.

"Very well, then. I will kill you and then change into her." The mimic rolled his eyes and moved in closer to strike.

Mitzi reached her hand inside her jeans pocket and maneuvered the drawstring bag open, carefully pinching a bit of the knotgrass powder. As the Mimic dad leaned over with the knife in his hand, she stretched her hand out in front of her and blew the biggest breath she could, sending the knotgrass powder into the air and toward their attacker.

The cloud of powder hit the Mimic directly in his face and he flew back onto the ground, pulling at his face as it started to shake and scream.

"Get up!" her father yelled. "We need to find something to contain this thing as soon as it morphs!" The two glanced around the hall and saw nothing that would work, so Mitzi ran out the front door to look in the yard. She could hear the beast yelling through his painful transition as she searched around the front of the house. "There!" she yelled at the sight of a garbage bin at the corner of the driveway. She ran up to it and popped the lid off. She pushed it to the ground, dumping stinking bags of household waste before snatching it up and running inside.

"Perfect!" her father yelled as he took the bin from her and stood ready, over the almost-completely-morphed pile of bubbling grey goo on the floor in front of him. "Here come those spines..." he said as the needle-arms came poking out of the blob. "Those are what we need to be careful with!"

"I know!" Mitzi said. "I nearly took a poke to the leg when I pushed that other one into the closet over there. They watched as the blob shook and bubbled and shrank to a rounded ball of goo. It started to shift and turn away from them, but Dad quickly covered it with the bin. "Kill us now you son of a…."

"Dad! Don't we need to weigh that down? Seems like it could easily get out of there…" Mitzi took a step away from the garbage can jail.

"Nope. Those puss bags can't move in the dark…lose all sense of direction. Useless beasts…" He kicked the bin.

"What do we do with them now?" she asked, feeling tired and a bit overwhelmed.

"We can deal with that in a bit. First, we better make sure that your mother and Rose handled that last one alright." Her father ran his fingers through his hair as he headed toward the kitchen.

Relief flooded through Mitzi as they entered the kitchen to find Rose standing by the sink and her mother sitting on top of an upside-down, kitchen garbage can in the middle of the room. Mitzi smiled at Rose and ran over to hug her mother. "Thank God this is over with…" Deb smiled at Mitzi and reached over and tucked her hair behind her ear. "I can't wait to hear how you figured all of this out, Mitz." Deb looked up at her husband and cocked her head to the side playfully. "What took you so long out there? We had to fight off a Mimic, you know…"

"I knew you two ladies could handle yourself," Dad said, chuckling. "Besides, Mitzi and I had two of them to deal with. One is nothing!"

"Nothing, my foot!" laughed Deb as she scooted off her garbage can chair. "Come on, guys… Let's get the others and get the heck out of here!"

"We're just going to leave these things here?" Rose asked with a look of absolute disgust on her face.

"No, no, no! Not at all," Dad said. "Once I make the call, The SHUT hazard management crew will be here within the hour to take care of those things and debrief the Halberts."

"Oh. Wow. I guess that makes sense then," Rose mumbled as they all left the kitchen to get the others.

Chapter Twenty-Four

By the time the group made it outside and onto the Halberts' porch, the sky had turned dark. Mitzi's father, mother, and Martin were huddled near the door with the three Halberts, explaining to them about the Hazard Crew that was on their way and what they could expect to happen over the next few hours.

Mitzi, Rose, and Finn sat on the top step, shoulder to shoulder, in silence...processing the afternoon's events.

"Holy crap. I can't even believe all of that just happened." Finn broke the silence.

"Did it, though?" asked Rose. "I keep thinking that I am gonna wake up any second and this was all just some strange dream, ya know?"

"I just don't know what it's gonna be like anymore." Mitzi thought out loud. "I mean...life can never be the same."

"Why?" Finn said with a laugh. "Do you mean just because we found out that your parents are the heads of a secret organization that hunts supernatural creatures, that we can't just continue living life like we did before? Pish Posh...of course we can!" He laughed and nudged Mitzi's shoulder.

"Oh. My. God." Rose dropped her head in her hands.

"What?" Finn and Mitzi asked in unison.

"I just don't think I will ever sleep again." Rose looked up. "I mean, Vampires, werewolves, ghosts, WRAITHS... DEMONS... SERIOUSLY?!"

Mitzi took a deep breath and thought for a moment. "It is some pretty crazy business, that's for sure. But, SHUT has been keeping the lid on all of it for so long, I don't really think we need to worry because SHUT will protect us like they always have. We are just going to have to get used to the fact that everything is just different now. There's no going back. We need to… What the…?" Mitzi stood as a car without headlights on came flying down the driveway in a dark dust storm of dirt and gravel. Finn and Rose stood up, too, unsure of how to react. They all stood staring as the car screeched to a halt just a few feet away.

"MR. MOORE!!!" Finn yelled as he slapped his hand to his forehead. "Why the heck is he just showing up now?"

The old man pushed open his door and as quickly as he could, hobbled up to the kids on the steps.

"Oh, my lord... Thank God you three are okay!" He was out of breath and his voice shook with emotion. "I would never be able to forgive myself if something happened..."

"What *did* happen to you, Mr. Moore?" Mitzi asked with a concerned look on her face.

"Yeah, are you okay?" added Rose.

Although it was dark outside, the kids could easily see the crimson red flush to Mr. Moore's face. "I... I..." He didn't want to say the words... "I fell asleep!!! I'm so sorry!!! I *am* 90-years-old, after all!"

And with that, the three young heroes hugged the old man as they all started to laugh.

EPILOGUE

Mitzi could hardly contain her excitement from her seat at the large table in the Den. Finn was nervously bouncing his legs up and down next to her and she could feel the vibration on the floor. Rose sat on her other side with a still confidence and warm smile. Mitzi looked at all of the other people seated around the giant table, only recognizing a few... Martin, and a few other 'lawyers' that she'd seen at her dad's office were there, and Mr. Moore was way down at the end of the table. Mitzi's mom sat directly across from her, looking proud and happy at the special occasion. Mitzi's dad stood to speak.

"Thank you all for coming tonight. Tonight, the Society for Hiding Undesirable Truths is making history by inducting the youngest members into our force...our youngest ever. I am honored to announce, after a unanimous vote by the Senior Cabinet, my daughter, Mitzi Clark, and her friends, Finn Cooper and Rose Brown, shall be hereby sworn in as full members of SHUT. I would now like to read a message from National headquarters...

"Just over one month ago, three young people saved several members of SHUT and three civilians from an extremely dangerous situation. It is quite rare in today's world for anyone to display such bravery when faced with new and terrifying truths. These three heroes also maintained our secrecy and were discreet in their amazing actions. Ms. Clark, Ms. Brown, and Mr. Cooper did not hesitate putting the needs of others in front of their own safety. They have exhibited every characteristic that we look for when recruiting our members. It is our great honor to welcome them, our youngest ever members, into our Society and pray for their ongoing safety in our daily hunt. Sincerely, President Dawson."

Cheers and clapping rang out through the Den. Dad lifted his hand into the air to silence the applause.

"There's a bit more…" He cleared his throat. "P.S. For stepping out of retirement and assisting our newest members, Mr. Herbert Moore, is hereby awarded the International Metal of Merit, our highest and most esteemed honor."

A roar of applause rang out throughout the Den a second time. Mr. Moore sat a bit taller in his chair and his eyes welled with tears.

"Mitzi, Rose, and Finn," Dad said. "Please stand to take your oath... Raise your right hand and repeat after me."

As Mitzi recited the oath, she felt a surge of pride.

"I, Mitzi Clark, do solemnly swear, to keep the Secrets of The Society for Hiding Undesirable Truths. I will protect these secrets with everything I have, up to and including, my life. I will honor the society code and protect our members and our secrets until the day I die."

"Welcome, our new Members of SHUT!" Dad yelled, and the shouts and applause were deafening, lasting for several minutes.

Over the next couple of hours, the three spent time meeting all the other members. They listened to story after story of missions, hunts, and creatures.

"Attention!" her dad yelled to quiet the group. "This has been quite an event but it's time that we must conclude our evening. We will exit the Den in small groups, starting with Team Elephant and then

Team Eagle." There was chatter from the crowd as the first lot went toward the exit.

Mitzi looked around for Mr. Moore and didn't see him anywhere. "Dad, where is Mr. Moore? Did you see him leave?" She found it odd that he would leave without saying goodbye.

"No, Mitz...I didn't see him leave. That is a bit odd…" he said as a member of Team Eagle came running toward them.

"Ben!" he shouted to Mitzi's father, out of breath. "I was escorting the team out and I noticed the storage room door was open. I went over to check it out and saw the lock had been pried open!"

"Do you know what was taken? This is not good," Ben asked as he scratched the back of his head.

"From what I could tell, the thief only took one item... The other cases look completely undisturbed. The thief took the Covenant Cube."

"Oh no." Ben's face grew serious. "This could be a big problem." He stood perfectly still, considering the next steps forward. "Seal up the storage room and check everyone before they leave. I have a feeling that the person who took it left a while ago."

"I'll get right on that," the man said as he left to follow his new orders.

Mitzi could feel a lump growing in her stomach. "Hey Dad…" she whispered. "What is the Covenant Cube?"

"You have so much to learn. The Covenant Cube is a very powerful weapon; it contains the blood of the Dark Trinity. Unleashing the power of the Dark Trinity would have grave consequences," he said, looking upset. "I will explain more later… Right now, I need to find Mr. Moore."

"You think that Mr. Moore took it, don't you?" Mitzi asked, but already knew his answer.

"Yes. Yes, I do," he said. "I just can't figure out what he could possibly need it for."

"Well…I guess it looks like we have another mystery on our hands," Mitzi said, glancing over at Rose and Finn, who were waiting to leave. "We best get started. If Mr. Moore needs our help, there is no time to waste."

"Just one minute, young lady." Ben cleared his throat. "You three may be new members of SHUT, and I am very proud of you. But you still have school starting tomorrow."

"Oh man," Finn complained. "This summer went by way too quickly."

"I was hoping Team Whale would have something more exiting to do than just homework this year," Rose blurted.

"We are more like team *beached* whale." Finn laughed at his own joke.

Mitzi did not want to go back to school. Learning Math and English seemed like such a waste of time now…regular schoolwork so trivial after discovering the existence of a whole supernatural world of monsters and creatures around them.

"I don't know how yet," Mitzi looked from friend to friend, "but we *will* find Mr. Moore and help clear his name. We owe it to him."

"I can see the headline now." Rose swished her hand through the air and did her best newscaster voice. "Team Whale Defeats the Dark Trinity, while recovering the Covenant Cube and rescues Mr. Moore…all before midterms."

Finn slapped his forehead. "Rose, you are so *extra*. Can't you just be serious? This is a big deal."

"Oh, I know it's a big deal, Finny. But, I mean, let's get real here." Rose's voice cracked with emotion. "How in the hell are we going to manage school and SHUT? This is all a bit much, don't you think? Mitzi?"

"Yes," Mitzi said matter-of-factly. "This is a bit much. It's all happening so fast. But just remember what *we* did. *We* stopped the mimics. *We* rescued my parents. We kept the secrets of SHUT safe. I am Mitzi Clark…and *we* are Team Whale…and as long as we have each other, we are unstoppable."

THE END

Made in the USA
Middletown, DE
24 November 2021

53245856R00132